# THE LIZARD
# OF OZ

## GOOSEBUMPS®
## HALL OF HORRORS

#1 CLAWS!

#2 NIGHT OF THE GIANT EVERYTHING

#3 SPECIAL EDITION: THE FIVE MASKS OF DR. SCREEM

#4 WHY I QUIT ZOMBIE SCHOOL

#5 DON'T SCREAM!

#6 THE BIRTHDAY PARTY OF NO RETURN

## GOOSEBUMPS® WANTED:
## THE HAUNTED MASK

## GOOSEBUMPS®
## MOST WANTED

#1 PLANET OF THE LAWN GNOMES

#2 SON OF SLAPPY

#3 HOW I MET MY MONSTER

#4 FRANKENSTEIN'S DOG

#5 DR. MANIAC WILL SEE YOU NOW

#6 CREATURE TEACHER: FINAL EXAM

#7 A NIGHTMARE ON CLOWN STREET

#8 NIGHT OF THE PUPPET PEOPLE

#9 HERE COMES THE SHAGGEDY

#10 THE LIZARD OF OZ

SPECIAL EDITION #1 ZOMBIE HALLOWEEN

SPECIAL EDITION #2 THE 12 SCREAMS OF CHRISTMAS

SPECIAL EDITION #3 TRICK OR TRAP

SPECIAL EDITION #4 THE HAUNTER

# GOOSEBUMPS®

Also available as ebooks

NIGHT OF THE LIVING DUMMY
DEEP TROUBLE
MONSTER BLOOD
THE HAUNTED MASK
ONE DAY AT HORRORLAND
THE CURSE OF THE MUMMY'S TOMB
BE CAREFUL WHAT YOU WISH FOR
SAY CHEESE AND DIE!
THE HORROR AT CAMP JELLYJAM
HOW I GOT MY SHRUNKEN HEAD
THE WEREWOLF OF FEVER SWAMP
A NIGHT IN TERROR TOWER
WELCOME TO DEAD HOUSE
WELCOME TO CAMP NIGHTMARE
GHOST BEACH
THE SCARECROW WALKS AT MIDNIGHT
YOU CAN'T SCARE ME!
RETURN OF THE MUMMY
REVENGE OF THE LAWN GNOMES
PHANTOM OF THE AUDITORIUM
VAMPIRE BREATH
STAY OUT OF THE BASEMENT
A SHOCKER ON SHOCK STREET
LET'S GET INVISIBLE!
NIGHT OF THE LIVING DUMMY 2
NIGHT OF THE LIVING DUMMY 3
THE ABOMINABLE SNOWMAN OF PASADENA
THE BLOB THAT ATE EVERYONE
THE GHOST NEXT DOOR
THE HAUNTED CAR
ATTACK OF THE GRAVEYARD GHOULS
PLEASE DON'T FEED THE VAMPIRE

## ALSO AVAILABLE:

IT CAME FROM OHIO!: MY LIFE AS A WRITER by R.L. Stine

# THE LIZARD
# OF OZ

## R.L. STINE

SCHOLASTIC INC.

Goosebumps book series created by Parachute Press, Inc.
Copyright © 2016 by Scholastic Inc.

ISBN 978-0-545-82549-8

10  9  8  7  6  5  4  3  2  1          16  17  18  19  20

Printed in the U.S.A.    40
First printing 2016

# WELCOME. YOU ARE MOST WANTED.

Hello, I'm R.L. Stine. I see you've found the Goosebumps office.

Let me ask you a question. Have you ever seen a real quicksand pit?

Well, guess what? You're standing in one!

Do you suddenly have a sinking feeling?

Ever hear the old expression "sink or swim"? I think you're about to do both!

Ha-ha. Don't worry. I'll get a rope and pull you out. Right after I have my lunch.

Hey, don't go anywhere, okay?

Only kidding. Here. Let me give you a hand. Come into my office.

I see you are admiring the WANTED posters on the wall. Those posters show the creepiest, crawliest, grossest Goosebumps characters of all time. They are the MOST WANTED characters from the MOST WANTED books.

That poster you are studying is of a very ugly

dude, a lizard from Australia we call "The Lizard of Oz."

One bite from this toothy reptile might change your life forever. Just ask Kate Lipton. She came a little too close one day and . . .

Well, Kate will tell you what one lizard bite can do. Once you read her story, you'll soon understand why The Lizard of Oz is MOST WANTED.

**1**

My name is Kate Lipton, and I just want to say that my parents are crazy. I'm twelve and my brother Freddy is ten, and I honestly feel like I'm the grown-up in our family.

What do I mean? Well, it's hard to know where to start.

Maybe I'll start with the Miniature Horse Petting Farm. That was our parents' latest brilliant idea. And by *brilliant*, I mean *stupid*.

They both had normal jobs. Mom was a reading teacher at Gooding Elementary School across town. And Dad was an accountant for a chain of pharmacies here in Middle Village, Pennsylvania.

But they decided those jobs were boring. They saved up their money. And one day, they announced their big plan to Freddy and me.

The four of us were sitting around the kitchen table. Dinner was over, but we were still finishing up bowls of frozen yogurt for dessert. "We're quitting our jobs," Dad said.

Freddy did a spit take with his yogurt, spraying the whole table. "You're *what*?"

Freddy thinks he's a comedian. He thinks it's hilarious to spit water or milk, and turn himself into a human geyser.

I don't know why Mom and Dad put up with it. Well, I *do* know. They're both crazy.

"What are you going to do now?" I asked. I'm the sensible one, remember?

"We bought twelve miniature horses," Dad said. Mom flashed him an approving smile. "We're going to sell miniature horses. Breed them and sell them."

"Doesn't that sound like fun?" Mom added.

"Fun?" I said.

"We'll make a ton of money," Dad said. "They're totally adorable. Once you see one, you have to own one."

"Where are we going to keep them?" Freddy asked. "Can I have one in my room?"

"We bought a farm to keep them on," Mom answered.

Freddy and I both gasped. "You mean we're *moving*?"

Mom shook her head. "No. We're staying in the house. We bought a farm to keep the horses on. Wait till you see it. You'll see how much fun it's going to be."

"We'll all pitch in and take care of them," Dad said.

4

"You mean we have to shovel up after them?" I asked.

Mom flashed me her Unhappy Look. "Kate, why do you always have to be so negative?"

*Because I'm not crazy?*

"You'll fall in love with them. I promise," Dad said.

Well . . . Freddy and I liked the little horses okay. They were cute and very sweet and funny.

But Mom and Dad couldn't sell any of them. After three months, they still had twelve miniature horses.

Middle Village is a pretty small town. And people just don't have room in their backyards for a miniature horse. We have a neighbor on the corner who has a pet pig named Jolly, and they keep Jolly in the house.

But you can't keep a miniature horse in the house. That would be cruel—for everybody.

So, they came up with a new idea. They decided to turn the farm into a miniature-horse petting farm. "We're not going to sell these wonderful animals," Dad announced. "We'll have huge crowds paying admission to come pet and feed them."

"And we'll give mini-horse rides to all the little kids," Mom said.

Guess what? That plan didn't work out, either.

See, you might want to pet *one* mini horse. That's kind of fun. But once you've petted one, you don't really want to pet eleven more.

5

Most petting zoos have a whole bunch of different animals to pet and feed. But we had only miniature horses. Bor-ing.

The crowds didn't come, and my parents were going broke. We couldn't even go on our annual summer vacation to the cabin at the lake. And Mom said when school started in the fall, we probably wouldn't shop for new school outfits. We'd probably have to make do with last year's clothes.

That's no problem for me. But Freddy grew at least two inches this summer, so he would look really dorky in his short jeans and tight shirts.

Then my parents had a "brilliant" new idea. Which is why we are all in Australia.

And if I tell you this idea, I swear you won't believe it.

I don't want to come right out and tell you their insane plan. I'll just give you a hint: We are halfway around the world in Queensland, Australia. That's a long way from Middle Village. And guess what we're doing? We're looking at lizards.

My parents have always been lizard freaks. They have an entire shelf of books about lizards. They have a big painting of lizards sunning on rocks in their bedroom. They love shows on PBS about lizards. And they even collected little salamanders for a while.

Australia, Dad says, is the place for lizards. I guess they have more lizards there than anywhere on earth.

So, my aunt Lydia loaned Mom and Dad the money for this trip. And here we are, spending all our time doing guess what? That's right. Looking at lizards.

Freddy the comedian keeps pointing at the ugly, warty creatures and saying, "That one

7

looks just like Kate when she wakes up in the morning." Or: "Look at those watery eyes. Just like Kate."

He's my brother and I love him. I just don't have the heart to break it to him that he's not funny.

Dad put a finger to his lips, motioning for Freddy to shut up. "Let's be serious," he said. "This is a serious place and we have serious work to do."

The serious place is the Queens Park Wildlife Preserve. They have so many weird animals in Australia. I'd love to see a dingo or an emu or a kangaroo.

Dad says maybe we'll get to those later. But we flew here for one reason—to check out the lizards.

"This is so fun," Mom said. She always says that when she sees that Freddy and I aren't having fun.

Don't get me wrong. I love visiting a country so far away. I'm just not happy that my parents might want to bring lizards back to Middle Village and start a lizard petting zoo or something.

Freddy and I were hanging back. "Come over here." Dad motioned with both hands. "You're not going to see lizards like this back home."

"I hope not!" Freddy exclaimed.

A low wire fence separated us from the lizards.

They sat sunning themselves on rocks or on the sandy shore of a narrow ribbon of water.

Dad pointed to the lizard guidebook in his hand. "See that one? That one is called a thorny devil. See? It has big, mean-looking pointed thorns poking out from all over its body."

"Eww, gross," I said.

"I think it's *cute*," Freddy said. He laughed. He knew the last thing you'd call that lizard is *cute*.

"The book says that Australia has seven hundred different kinds of lizards," Dad said. "More lizards than anywhere in the world."

"A fun fact," Mom said.

Dad stared at her. "What's that supposed to mean?"

She shrugged.

"What's that one?" I asked, pointing to a small lizard raising its head to the sun.

Dad checked through the book. "It's a blue-tongue lizard. It says they're very tame."

Freddy gave me a push. "Go put your finger in its mouth. See if it's really tame."

"Go put your *head* in its mouth," I said.

He grinned. "Dare me?"

Mom pulled her baseball cap lower on her forehead. "That sun is strong." She turned to me. "Kate, can you picture these amazing lizards back home on our farm?"

I didn't get a chance to answer. Dad interrupted. "Whoa. Look at that one coming toward us. See its beard? It's a bearded dragon lizard."

I turned in time to see the lizard begin to hurtle toward us. It was at least two feet long. It snapped its jaws once. Twice. It didn't slow down as it approached the low fence.

"Look out!" Dad cried. "It's going to jump the fence! It's going to ATTACK!"

**3**

Freddy and I yelped and stumbled back from the fence. I think my heart stopped beating for at least ten seconds.

Of course, the mean-looking lizard didn't even come near the fence.

Dad was laughing his head off, and Mom was shaking her head, punching his shoulder.

Big joke.

I told you my parents are crazy. And they're both big babies, too. Dad loves scaring Freddy and me, and we almost always fall for his dumb jokes.

Don't ask me why. I guess it's because he's Dad and we expect him to be a grown-up.

"We'll have to build a good fence on the farm," Dad said, turning serious. "We're lucky we have that nice stream that cuts through the middle of it. The lizards will like that."

"Don't lizards like to live in a swamp?" I asked.

"Do you really think it's warm enough for lizards in Middle Village?"

Mom and Dad both blinked. I don't think they'd even thought about it. They just get these wild ideas in their heads.

"We'll bring the lizards indoors in the winter," Mom said. "Cousin Arnie has that empty storage warehouse near his house."

"I'm so pumped!" Dad exclaimed, grinning. "I love these lizards. Can you imagine what an attraction our lizard farm will be? It will be unique. Nothing like it anywhere."

"People will come from all over the state," Mom said. "No. All over the country. We'll get it talked about on travel websites and in travel guides. It will be like SeaWorld or something."

I love their enthusiasm. They get so excited about these plans. I always hate to bring them back to earth by asking practical questions.

"Can you just buy lizards here in Australia and bring them back to our country?" I asked.

Dad shook his head. "This is a wildlife preserve. They don't sell any of their animals. We have to go to an export company. There's a lot of legal stuff we have to do. It may take a while, but—"

Dad stopped midsentence. Suddenly, he shut his eyes. He wrinkled up his nose. His mouth dropped open, and he let out a loud sneeze. Then another sneeze. Then another sneeze that shook his whole body.

No. My dad wasn't allergic to lizards. He was having one of his weird sneezing fits.

Mom, Freddy, and I took a step back and watched him. But we weren't alarmed or anything. He has these wild sneezing attacks all the time.

It's kind of funny. The poor guy sneezes eight or ten times in a row until his face is red and he can't catch his breath. Then it stops just as suddenly as it starts.

Dr. Wilkinson can't explain it. He sent Dad for studies at the university health center. And no one there could explain it, either. They told him it wasn't dangerous. Actually, it always makes Freddy and me laugh.

Dad sneezed a few more times, then mopped his face with a tissue. "Barry, you're scaring the lizards!" Mom exclaimed.

"Excuse me." We turned to see an older man standing behind us. He had bright blue eyes and a short, white stubble of beard on his wrinkled face. He wore a white suit and had a wide-brimmed straw hat pulled down over his forehead.

"I couldn't help overhearing . . ." he said.

"My sneezing fit?" Dad said. "No problem. It happens a lot."

The man tilted his hat back. It left a red line on his pale forehead. His blue eyes studied Dad intensely. "No. You misunderstand me. I heard your talk about buying lizards."

"Do you work for the wildlife preserve?" Mom asked him.

"Not anymore," he said. "But I think I have something for you. A lizard you might be interested in. Something very rare and very special."

Mom and Dad exchanged glances. "Can we see it?" Mom asked.

The man nodded. "Yes. Follow me."

We all began walking along the path that led to the exit.

"Does this lizard bite?" Freddy asked.

A strange smile spread over the man's face. "Oh yes. It bites. It definitely bites."

# 4

"I am Dr. Clegg," the old man said. He took off his hat and placed it on a hook on the back of the door. He smoothed his mane of white hair.

We had followed him to his lab, a few blocks from the wildlife preserve. As we walked, white ibis birds crossed our path, crisscrossing in front of us. They were tall birds with spindly legs and long, pointed bills. They walked awkwardly, as if they were on stilts.

"Ibises are the pigeons of Australia," Dr. Clegg told us. "Comical birds, aren't they?"

The walls of his lab were white. Bright ceiling lights made the whole room glow. I spotted a row of cages against the back wall.

"I have a lizard you might be interested in," Dr. Clegg said. He motioned us toward the cages. "It definitely would be a popular attraction. Perhaps the star of your lizard farm?"

"Whoa." Freddy let out a cry as we stepped near. We were staring at a long, ugly, mean-faced green lizard. It had bumps down its back like shark fins. A single horn poked up from the top of its scaly head.

It raised itself as we approached the cage. And snapped two rows of jagged teeth. Its nostrils pulsed in and out, and its weird yellow eyes locked on us.

"It looks like a dinosaur!" I blurted out.

Dr. Clegg nodded, smiling. "Yes. A creature from a horror movie. Only smaller. He weighs about fifty pounds."

"Mean face," Freddy murmured, leaning close to the cage.

The lizard snapped its teeth again. It swung its long, bumpy tail from side to side.

"I don't think it's in my lizard book," Dad said. "What is it called?"

"You won't find it in a guidebook," the old man said. "It's too rare. It's a Tasmanian cobra lizard. There are so few of them, they are very valuable."

Freddy lowered his face close to the cage and peered in. "He looks mean. What does he eat?"

"Anything he wants to!" Dr. Clegg replied.

Silence for a moment. Then we all realized he was making a joke, and we laughed.

The lizard suddenly made a *heeheeheee* wheezing sound, as if it was laughing, too.

"Actually, he'll be very happy on a diet of crickets," Dr. Clegg said. "He looks ferocious, but he's not much of a meat eater. And these lizards are actually quite timid—unless provoked."

I heard a crash behind us. I spun around to see a young woman in a pale blue uniform, standing over a bunch of metal trays she had just dropped.

"Sorry, Dr. Clegg," she said, blushing. She bent down to pick up the trays.

"No problem, Miss Morris," he said. "Those specimen trays are slippery."

He turned back to us. "Miss Morris is my lab assistant. I don't know what I'd do without her."

I glanced back at her. To my surprise, she seemed to be signaling to me, motioning to me with one hand.

When Dr. Clegg turned, she quickly went back to collecting the trays.

Dr. Clegg tapped the top of the wooden cage. "It's a very easy lizard to take care of," he told my parents. "I imagine you live in a fairly warm place? You have water on your farm for the lizards to swim in and use?"

Mom and Dad nodded. "Unless it needs really hot weather all the time, it should be okay in Middle Village," Mom said.

Dad blinked. I could see he suddenly had a

thought. "Are you thinking of selling this lizard to us, Dr. Clegg?"

A thin smile spread over the old man's face, making his cheeks crinkle up. "I'm going to sell you something better than that," he said.

# 5

Dr. Clegg walked over to his assistant and gave her some instructions. She nodded and left the room, carrying the stack of trays in both hands.

"Do you think I could bring a lizard to school?" Freddy asked Mom and Dad. "Wouldn't that be cool?"

Dad laughed. "Look at the ugly face. Do you want to scare everyone to death?"

"Yes," Freddy answered.

Mom and Dad are so crazy, they'd probably let Freddy take the creature to school on a leash or something. I knew I had to speak up. "It probably would be too scary for the lizard," I told Freddy. "He might go berserk or have a heart attack or something."

I suddenly thought of Adele Bender, a girl at school who pretended to be my friend but really wasn't. Adele always had to win, no matter what. She thought everything was a competition. And she was always desperate to beat me and come out on top.

She always has to know what score I get on every quiz, just to see if she beat me or not. And when we have our tennis lesson, she *kills* the ball. I mean, she *slams* it at me as if we're playing dodgeball instead of tennis.

Last year, I invited twelve kids to my birthday party. So she invited fourteen to hers. See? Everything is a contest with Adele.

I pictured the look on her face if I showed up with this amazingly weird and valuable lizard at school. I'd get so much attention, she'd seriously *die*. Ha-ha.

I was still thinking about Adele when Miss Morris returned to the room. She carried a small glass box in front of her in both hands.

She handed the box carefully to Dr. Clegg. Once again, I got the idea she was signaling to me, this time with her eyes.

Dr. Clegg carried the box over to us. In the cage, the Tasmanian cobra lizard lowered its head to the cage floor and shut its yellow eyes.

"This is better than selling you a full-grown lizard," the old man said. He raised the glass box, and I could see a pale white egg inside. "For one thing, it will be easier for you to get it safely through the airport and through customs."

We all squinted at it.

"It's a lizard egg?" Freddy asked.

Dr. Clegg nodded. "They take only a few weeks to hatch. I can give you complete instructions. This is the only egg I have right now. But I am willing to sell it to you to start your lizard collection."

Mom and Dad gazed at it wide-eyed. They really do look like children when they get excited like this.

"A Tasmanian cobra lizard could make us famous!" Dad exclaimed.

Mom finally asked a sensible question. "How much will it cost us?"

Dr. Clegg flashed his thin smile again. "We can talk about that," he said. "I'm sure we can agree on a price."

A million thoughts whirred through my head. *Shouldn't my parents do some more research on this lizard? Shouldn't they do a little research on Dr. Clegg? At least Google him?*

*Do they really think they can just carry the lizard egg on the plane? Won't they get in some kind of trouble with the airport security people?*

I wondered if any of these questions crossed their minds as they gazed so excitedly at the little egg.

I wandered away as the three adults talked about the price. Miss Morris stood in the doorway to the next room, half-hidden in shadow. She waved frantically to me. "Here. Over here," she whispered.

I hesitated. Then I walked over to her.

She grabbed my wrist. "Listen to me, mate," she whispered. Her eyes were on Dr. Clegg across the room. "Don't take that egg. I'm warning you. Don't take that egg."

"Wh-why not?" I stammered.

But her eyes suddenly grew wide with fright. I turned and saw Dr. Clegg staring at us. And when I turned back, Miss Morris had vanished into the other room.

I saw Dr. Clegg shaking hands first with my mom, then with my dad. I didn't have to hear the news. I could see they had a deal. And I knew my family was the proud owner of an egg that would hatch out a Tasmanian cobra lizard.

Mom and Dad looked so happy, I thought their faces might burst. I mean, their gleeful grins made them look like kids who were just told they were going to Disney World or had won a million-dollar prize.

I wanted to be happy about the lizard egg, too. But Miss Morris had ruined it for me. I could tell she was serious. She wasn't playing some kind of cruel joke.

If only she'd had a chance to explain her warning.

Freddy was down on the floor in front of the lizard cage. He poked a finger in and touched the sleeping lizard on the top of the head. "Hey, he feels warm," he reported. "Lizards usually feel cold."

"You're right," Dr. Clegg said. "Lizards are cold-blooded. That means they take on the temperature of their surroundings. That's why they spend so much time sunning themselves."

He pulled out a small pad and wrote a note to himself. "I'm going to send you a complete study of the Tasmanian cobra lizard as soon as you get home. I'm also going to give you my hotline number. There is a big time difference between Australia and the United States. But you can call me any time of the day with any questions or problems."

Dad held the glass box up to his face and peered in at the egg. "That will be a big help," he said. "I can't thank you enough, Dr. Clegg."

"Well, do keep in touch," the old man said, walking us to the door. "And I will want to see photos as soon as this little creature hatches out of there."

And then we were back out on the street. Mom and Dad couldn't stop chattering about what a lucky day it was and how the family lizard farm was going to be a huge hit.

Mom tucked the egg into her bag and carried the bag carefully in front of her in both hands as we made our way back to our hotel.

That night, I dreamed I was in some kind of big grocery store that had only eggs. Tall shelves of eggs—hundreds of eggs—all around. And I stood with a grocery cart and waited. I was just waiting for the eggs to start hatching. But they never did. Nothing happened. And I woke up feeling disappointed and frustrated.

I don't usually remember boring dreams like that. But I remembered that one.

And I was still thinking about it at the airport in Sydney as we boarded the plane for home. Mom sat in the row behind us. Dad sat between Freddy and me, and he kept the egg in its glass box on his lap. He didn't want to let it out of his sight.

Dad helped Freddy tighten his seat belt. "You know, a lot of times Australia is called Oz," he told us. "That's because an abbreviation for Australia is *Aus*. And people here pronounce that as *Oz*."

"And Sydney is sometimes called the Emerald City," Mom chimed in from behind us. "Like the city in *The Wizard of Oz*."

"That's right," Dad said. "So . . . guess what I have in my lap here. The *Lizard* of Oz!" He laughed at his own joke.

"That's lame," I said.

"I don't care," Dad replied. "It's funny."

Freddy and I laughed, too. Just to make him feel good.

We didn't know that the lizard inside that egg was no laughing matter. We didn't know that it was about to bring nothing but screaming horror into our lives.

# 7

I forgot to mention that we live in a creepy old house in the middle of two vacant lots. I didn't mention it because I don't like to think about it.

Mom and Dad bought the house because it reminded them of a haunted house they saw in a scary movie they went to on their first date.

Seriously.

They have big plans to fix the whole house up and make everything shiny and new. But, as I said, my parents have so many plans and ideas, they don't get around to a lot of them.

Well, they did work on some rooms, like the living room and the kitchen and our bedrooms. But it's a very big house, and most of it is your basic ruin. A bunch of rooms are shut off. We never even look inside them.

I'm telling you all this because, as soon as we got home, Mom and Dad cleared all the junk out of a spare bedroom in the back of the house on the first floor. They had it painted immediately, and they put up shelves.

And Dad said it was his hatching room. His lizard lab. He bought several glass cases to hold lizards in when they hatched and a bunch of other equipment he thought he might need when he buys more lizards.

I followed Dad as he carried the egg in its glass box into the hatching room. "This is exciting," he said, clicking the new ceiling light on.

"Did Dr. Clegg e-mail you all the instructions?" I asked.

"Not yet," Dad said.

"We've been home a week," I told him. "He should have sent them by now."

Dad shook his head. "Kate, you're such a worrier."

"*Someone* around here has to worry," I said.

For some reason, that made him laugh.

He carried the glass box to the larger case where he planned to keep the egg. A small space heater behind the case sent billowing hot air over the glass.

Dad started to lift the egg from the little box.

"Can I hold it? Just for a second?" I asked.

He hesitated. "I guess." He handed me the egg.

I cupped it between my hands. I held it against my palms. I hoped maybe I could feel something moving inside the egg.

But no. It just felt like an egg.

I handed it back to Dad. I realized I'd been holding my breath the whole time. I let it out in a long whoosh.

Dad held the egg carefully between his hands. "I'm going to keep it in this heated case—" he started. But then his expression changed.

His eyes bulged. He made a choking sound.

"Dad—what's wrong?" I cried.

"The egg. It ... it's ..." he stammered. "I can feel the lizard moving in there. It ... It's banging against the shell. I think ... I think ... Oh, wow! Here it comes! It's bursting out, Kate. Here it comes!"

**8**

I gasped and took a step back.

The egg quivered between Dad's hands.

"Get ready," Dad said. "Get ready to catch the lizard when it jumps out."

I raised both hands. My heart started to pound. My whole body tensed.

Dad burst out laughing. "Gotcha again," he said. "Did you really believe me? This lizard isn't going to hatch for at least two more weeks."

"Aaarrrgh!" I let out a scream. I bunched my fists tight. I wanted to punch my dad really hard. But I held myself back. I didn't want to make him drop the egg.

"How funny are your jokes?" I said. "Not!"

He laughed some more. "What's funny, Kate, is that you always fall for them."

I grumbled under my breath. Does everyone have a dad who is constantly playing babyish tricks on them? I don't think so.

Dad had spread a layer of sand over the bottom of the glass tank. He carefully lowered the egg into the sand. Then he adjusted the heater behind the tank.

"It's nice and warm and comfy in there," he said. "Our little friend will be popping out very soon."

I raised my phone and flashed a selfie of me and the egg beside me. I couldn't wait to show it to everyone at school. Ms. Arnold, my teacher, was a science freak. I knew she'd love the whole lizard story.

The next afternoon, in Ms. Arnold's class, I projected photos from Australia onto the wall. I heard a lot of oohs and aahs from the kids as they looked at the many kinds of lizards. The bearded lizards were a huge favorite. Some kids didn't think they were real.

I finished with my selfie of me and the egg. I talked about how my dad bought the egg and soon it would hatch a Tasmanian cobra lizard.

"That is so interesting," Ms. Arnold said, staring at the egg. "Kate, you will have to give us daily reports on what is happening with that egg. I think we all want to see what comes out when that egg cracks open."

That's when Adele Bender interrupted. I knew she would. I told you she's totally competitive with me. I knew she couldn't stand to see me get all this attention from Ms. Arnold and from the rest of the class.

"I know what will come out of that egg," Adele said. "Egg yolk!"

A few kids laughed.

Ms. Arnold narrowed her eyes at Adele. "What do you mean?"

"I mean, look at it," Adele said. Yes, she had a sneer on her face, her top lip curled up almost to her perfect nose. "That egg came from the supermarket. The whole thing is a fake."

Everyone started talking at once.

I knew Adele would say something like that. She always did.

Did I mention one way that she always comes out on top? She's a lot prettier than I am. She looks a lot like one of those magazine models with creamy skin, really high cheekbones, cat-shaped blue eyes, and long, wavy reddish hair to die for.

I don't want to talk about *my* hair. It looks like the kind of string they make floor mops out of. So I'm admitting it right now. Adele wins in the awesome-looking department.

But *no way* she could win on lizards.

It took Ms. Arnold a while to get everyone settled down. Adele remained with her arms crossed tightly in front of her, her mouth locked in a scowl.

"The egg is real," I said quietly. "Everyone

knows I went to Australia. Those lizards in my photos are all real, and they can only be found in Australia."

"The egg is real, too," Adele said. "You can make scrambled eggs out of it because it's a regular egg from the supermarket."

"You're crazy!" I cried. "You don't know what you're saying, Adele. You just think—"

I didn't get to finish my sentence because the bell rang. Everyone jumped up and began shoving things into their backpacks and talking and laughing.

I didn't move from the front of the room. Adele didn't move, either. She just sat there at her desk, staring at me. Challenging me.

And that's when I made a big mistake. That's when I invited her to come over to my house and see the egg for herself.

What was I thinking?

"I forgot how old your house is," Adele said as we walked up the front lawn. She kicked at a clump of dandelions. "These are probably pretty old weeds, too."

"We've been away," I said. "That's why the grass hasn't been mowed."

"We have a gardener who does it," Adele said.

We walked along the side of the house. We had to step around a rake and a shovel my dad had left on the ground. The garage door was open. Cartons were stacked everywhere. There was no room for the car in the garage.

I could see Adele taking in every messy detail. I knew she wanted to tell me what slobs my parents are and how her house is shiny new and neat.

"Your parents don't have jobs, do they?" she said.

She really wasn't a friend. Why had I asked her to come over? Just to prove I wasn't lying about the egg?

"You know we had a mini-horse farm," I said. "I brought the whole class there once, remember?"

She nodded. "They were cute."

"My parents have big plans for the lizards," I said. I opened the kitchen door and motioned for her to come in.

"Hey, I'm home!" I shouted.

No reply.

"Guess no one's home," I said.

The dirty breakfast dishes were still on the table. Adele made a sniffing sound. "What's that smell?"

"My dad had sardines for breakfast," I said. "He's totally weird."

"My parents are weird, too," Adele said. "They're probably a lot weirder than your parents."

See? She has to win at *everything*!

We dropped our backpacks against the wall. "Would you like a snack or something?" I asked.

Adele shook her head. "Not really." She pointed. "Is that your living room?"

I led the way down the short hall to the living room. "This is one of the rooms my parents fixed up. Most of the house still needs a lot of work. Would you believe my parents like to pretend they live in a haunted house?"

Adele didn't answer. I glimpsed something move quickly at her feet. Suddenly, her eyes bulged. Her mouth dropped open and she screamed.

"What *was* that? Did you see it? It ran right over my shoes!"

"I saw it," I said. "I think—"

"The lizard!" she screeched. "Kate, it's the lizard! It's running loose!"

# 10

She tilted back her head and started to scream.

I grabbed her shoulders to try to calm her down. "Adele, listen to me. Adele, take a breath. Don't panic."

She finally stopped. Breathing hard, she stared at me.

I laughed. "I think it was a mouse."

She swallowed. "A mouse?"

I nodded. "This old house is filled with mice. They mostly live in the empty rooms we don't use. But we were away for three weeks. In Australia, remember? And they've gotten a lot braver."

Adele's whole body shuddered. "I hate mice. They totally creep me out."

"Dad keeps promising to call an exterminator," I said. "But he's been busy trying to buy more lizards."

"Lizards," Adele repeated. "The egg. I almost forgot." She swept back her perfect coppery hair. "You said I could see the lizard egg. Where is it?"

I pointed down the back hall. "Mom and Dad set up a special hatching room. But they're not home. I don't think I can show it to you."

"I *knew* it!" Adele cried. "I knew the whole thing was a fake."

"No. Really—" I said.

"I was right," she insisted, her blue eyes flashing. "There *is* no egg. There is no lizard egg at all—*is* there!"

"Yes, there is a lizard egg," I said through gritted teeth. "I'm not a liar, Adele. But I don't think my parents would want me to show it to anyone unless one of them was here."

She sighed. "I just want to look at it. I won't touch it, Kate." She made a face. "Yuck. I don't want to touch it."

My mind whirred. I couldn't decide what to do. If I didn't show it to her, she'd tell everyone at school that she came to my house and there was no egg.

"Promise you won't try to pick it up or anything?" I said finally.

She raised her right hand. "Promise."

"Okay," I said. "I'll show it to you. I'll prove you are wrong."

I led the way down the hall. "Careful," I warned. "Some of the floorboards in this hall are loose."

The boards squeaked under our shoes. I suddenly had a heavy feeling of dread in the pit of my stomach. I knew I was taking a risk.

But . . . if we just looked at the egg resting in the glass tank, what could happen?

I stopped at the door to the hatching room. I took a deep breath. Then I pulled open the door.

And a horrifying, deafening cry made both of us gasp.

# 11

Adele grabbed me and squeezed my shoulders. Her eyes were wide with fright. "Wh-what was *that*?" she stammered.

I laughed. "It's Screech."

She let go of me. "Screech?"

"Yes," I said. "Screech. My dad's macaw." I pulled her into the room.

The big red-and-blue bird hopped up and down excitedly on his wooden perch. He tilted his feathery head to one side, ruffled his big red wings—and let out another deafening shriek.

Adele pressed her hands to her ears. "Why does he do that?"

"Gets excited, I guess. It's kind of boring being a macaw."

Adele frowned. "Why does your dad own a macaw?"

I shrugged. "Why does he do *anything*? I told you, both of my parents are seriously weird."

Adele tossed back her hair again. She gazed around the room. Her eyes stopped at the glass case on the long worktable. "Is that it?"

I nodded. "Dad is setting this room up as a lab and a workroom. You know. A place to get the lizards ready before we move them to the farm."

Adele crossed the room to the worktable. "I just want to look at the lizard egg and get out of here," she said. "No offense, Kate, but your house gives me the deep creeps."

*No offense? Really?*

I wanted to insult her back. "I never knew you scare so easily, Adele."

She squinted at me. "I wasn't scared. Just startled. First, a mouse attacks me in the living room. Then a parrot tries to make me deaf."

I grinned. "I know. It's like living in a wildlife preserve."

She leaned over the glass case and peered down at the egg. "Just as I said, Kate. It looks like an ordinary egg resting on sand."

"It's a lizard egg. Believe me," I said. "It's a little bigger than a hen's egg. And it's heavier. My dad let me hold it once."

She squinted down at it. "You're joking, right?"

I gritted my teeth again. "No way."

Why would I lie to her about this? Did she really think I made the whole lizard story up just to get attention in school?

I decided it was a big mistake bringing Adele home with me. And then I went ahead and made *another* big mistake . . .

"Can you take it out so I can see it better?" she asked.

"No way," I replied. "Come on, Adele. You promised you just wanted to look at it."

"But I can't really look at it in the sand. Under the glass. Just for a second, Kate. I just want to see it up close."

"I . . . don't think so." My hands suddenly felt cold and wet. I knew it was a very bad idea.

So why did I do it?

Just to make her stop calling it a fake? To make her stop calling me a liar?

Adele begged one more time.

I let out a long breath. Then I bumped her out of the way and leaned over the worktable.

Carefully . . . Carefully, I lowered both hands into the glass case. I could feel my heartbeat start to race. My hands were actually trembling.

I wrapped my fingers gently around the egg. It felt warm against my skin. Slowly, I lifted it out of the case.

Adele's eyes grew wide as I held the egg up close to her. "Can you feel anything moving around inside it?"

"No," I said. "Not at all. It must be too soon."

My hand felt wet against the hard eggshell.

"Are you satisfied, Adele?" I said. "Did you get a good look at it?"

"Let me just hold it for a second," she said.

She reached for the egg—and it slid out of my hand.

I let out a cry as the egg hit the hard floor with a loud *craaaack*.

I stared in horror as the shell cracked and shattered, and yellow goo oozed out around it on the floor.

Adele pressed her hands against her face and began to shriek at the top of her lungs: "I'm so sorry! I'm so sorry!"

But was that a pleased smile I saw cross her face?

I couldn't move. I couldn't breathe. I stared down at the yellow puddle of yolk as it spread over the floor.

How could this happen? How could I ruin *everything*?

I wanted to scream. I wanted to disappear. If only I could go back in time . . . back in time just one minute.

"Oh . . . oh . . . oh . . ." Low moans escaped my mouth.

"I'm so sorry!" Adele cried. "I'm so sorry!"

And then I turned—and saw my dad standing in the doorway, his eyes on the broken egg.

43

# 12

"Oh, Dad—" I choked out. I tried to say more, but the words wouldn't come.

"I'm so sorry!" Adele cried. She grabbed my hand and squeezed it.

Dad took two steps into the room—and burst out laughing.

"Dad—what's so funny? Are you okay?" I demanded. "Dad?"

He laughed till he was red in the face. Shaking his head, he laughed until tears rolled down his cheeks.

Adele and I gaped at him, our mouths hanging open.

*Has he lost his mind?* That's the thought I had. *Has the sight of the destroyed egg made him crazy?*

He finally stopped laughing. "Sorry," he murmured, wiping tears off his face with both hands. "Sorry, girls. It was a mean joke."

"Joke?" I said in a trembling whisper. "Joke?"

He nodded. "I switched the eggs this morning. That's an egg from the fridge." He started to laugh again.

I dove for him and wrapped my hands around his neck. "I . . . I could *strangle* you!" I stammered.

"You should have seen the looks on your faces," Dad said.

"I had *two* heart attacks!" I cried. "I couldn't breathe at all. Seriously." I shook him by the neck. "You and your stupid jokes!"

"I was going to play the joke on you and Freddy later, after dinner," he said. "But you two beat me to it."

Adele sank back against the worktable. Her face was pale, and she held her stomach. "I think I'm going to be sick," she murmured.

"I'll get you a glass of water," Dad said.

She shook her head. "Just let me catch my breath. That was quite a scare, Mr. Lipton."

I rolled my eyes. "That's what life around here is like all the time," I told Adele.

"Stop complaining. You love it," Dad said.

I shook my head. "Who says?" I glanced down at the puddle of egg at my feet. "That was the meanest joke you ever pulled, Dad."

He grinned. I realized he took that as a compliment.

"Do you want to see the real lizard egg?" he asked Adele. "I put it in the warmer over here."

He walked to a shelf behind us. I saw that he had a new piece of equipment. It was silvery and rectangular and a little bigger than a toaster.

Dad rubbed his hand over the top. "This new warmer protects the egg from the air," he said. "And it keeps it at a good temperature."

Adele and I hung back. "Is this another joke?" Adele asked. She had her hands clenched tightly in front of her.

"Yes. Is something going to come flying out at us when you open it?" I asked.

Dad shook his head. "No. I'm serious now. No more jokes. This lizard is too valuable. And too important to our family's future."

I moved closer. Adele didn't budge.

Dad lifted the top of the warmer. Then he reached in and carefully lifted the egg out. "This is the egg of a very rare Tasmanian cobra lizard," he told Adele. "Kate has probably told you all about it."

Adele took a few reluctant steps closer to the egg. She squinted hard at it. "It has speckles on it," she said.

"See? It doesn't look like a regular egg," I said. "The shape is a little different, too."

"It's going to hatch soon," Dad said. He petted the egg with one finger. "This little guy is going to be the star of our new lizard farm."

He turned and started to lower the egg back into the warmer.

"Thanks for showing it to me, Mr. Lipton," Adele said.

I saw Dad's nose twitch. The egg appeared to bounce in his hand. Dad's eyes shut suddenly.

He tilted back his head—and let out a loud, explosive sneeze.

Then another. Then another.

I gasped. *Another sneezing attack!*

A sneeze exploded from his mouth and nose in a deafening roar.

I watched, frozen in horror, as the lizard egg flew from his hand.

"Oh nooooo." A moan escaped my throat.

The egg sailed across the room and smashed hard into the side of the worktable. It dropped to the floor. Jagged lines spread over the shell. And it cracked open with a sick *craaaaack* like shattering glass.

His empty hand still raised in front of him, Dad sneezed again. Again.

And Adele and I stared down at the broken egg . . . waiting. Waiting to see what would crawl out.

# 13

Dad pulled a tissue from his pants pocket and mopped at his nose.

A hush fell over the room. I could feel the blood pulsing at my temples.

The cracked egg lay on its side at our feet, a ragged hole in it. Green yolk, the color of pea soup, poured out and formed a thick puddle on the floor.

No one moved. No one blinked.

Waiting. We were waiting for the lizard to appear, to poke its head out, to come tumbling out with the oozing green yolk.

But no.

The egg didn't tilt or crack more. No creature came scampering out. The thick liquid stopped dripping from the shell.

Nothing moved. Nothing.

"Dad," I whispered, finally finding my voice. I grabbed his sleeve. "Dad, please tell me this was another one of your jokes. Please."

Dad shook his head sadly. He avoided my eyes. "Not a joke, Kate," he murmured.

I let go of his shirtsleeve. He gazed down at the green mess on the floor. "The joke is my career," he said bitterly. "All of our big plans. Ruined by a sneeze. That's the joke."

"But, Dad—" I started.

He spun away. Head down, muttering to himself, he slunk toward the door.

"Dad, maybe that guy in Australia has more lizard eggs," I called after him.

But he disappeared out the door without saying another word.

I stood there for a moment, staring at the empty doorway, trying to catch my breath. I forced back the urge to burst into tears. But in that moment, I realized this was one of the saddest moments of my life.

Adele stood beside me, biting her bottom lip, her hands tensed into tight fists at her sides. "I'm so sorry," she whispered. "I guess I'd better go."

I didn't say anything. I didn't know what to say.

If I hadn't brought Adele home, would any of this have happened? Was it all my fault?

I led Adele back to the kitchen. She picked up her backpack and swung it onto her shoulders. "Sorry," she murmured again. It seemed to be the word of the day.

"See you in school," she said. I held the kitchen

door open for her and watched her walk away until she vanished around the side of the house.

Did I feel horribly sad? Yes.

Did I feel horribly guilty? Yes.

I decided to help Dad and clean up the mess on the floor of the hatching room. I grabbed a roll of paper towels from the kitchen counter and found a trash bag under the sink.

I carried them to the hatching room. A faint sour smell already floated over the room from the spilled egg yolks.

I dropped to my knees, grabbed a wad of paper towels, and began to mop up the yellow yolk from the refrigerator egg. Some of it stuck to the floor, and I had to rub hard to get it up.

*One good thing*, I thought. *After what happened today, Adele will never want to come here again.*

I dumped the broken shell and yellow yolk into the trash bag. Then I moved to the green lizard goo.

Still on my knees, I lifted the broken egg and began to swing it into the trash bag.

I jumped when I felt the shell bounce in my hand. "Whoa!" I cried out in shock. I saw something poke out. A tiny leg?

I raised the shell closer, squinting hard at it. Something wiggled. Another leg poked out. And then I gasped as a tiny creature fell out of the shell and bounced to the floor.

50

# 14

I was already on my knees. I dropped lower to see it better.

The thing was a little bigger than a grape. I couldn't see its head. The whole creature was covered in stubby black hair. It rolled over a few times. Then it pulled itself up onto four spindly legs.

I lowered my head almost to the floor. My whole body was trembling, with excitement, I guess.

Squinting hard, I saw a stub of a head with two tiny pinprick black eyes. The head bobbed up and down as the creature tested its legs.

*It doesn't look anything at all like a lizard,* I thought. *Is this really what a newly hatched lizard looks like?*

I jerked my head up as the tiny creature suddenly spun in a circle. Its legs flew out from under it, and it bounced on the floor. It froze for a few seconds, as if trying to figure out why it fell. Then, slowly, it raised itself on its slender legs.

"Dad is going to be so happy," I told myself. I reached into my jeans pocket for my phone. I wanted to snap some photos. But I remembered that my phone was charging up in my room.

The lizard looked like a fat, hairy bee. Its eyes were tinier than poppy seeds on its lump of a head. It steadied itself and began to walk again, slowly and carefully this time.

I glanced around the room. I knew I had to pick the lizard up and put it somewhere safe. But where? Would it stay in the glass case with the sand?

I watched it walk through the green puddle of yolk from the shattered egg. Its tiny head sniffed at pieces of the shell. Sticky green yolk stuck to its spindly legs, but it kept walking slowly but steadily until it stepped out of the puddle.

The hairy little lizard lowered its head and began to pick up speed as it walked in a straight line. I gazed in front of it and realized where it was going.

At first, I thought I was gazing at a black spot of dirt on the floor. But as it came into focus, I saw that it was a dead ant.

"Whoa." I uttered a sharp cry as the lizard darted up to the ant, lowered its head, opened tiny jaws—and snapped the ant into its mouth.

The jaws worked quickly. I heard noisy chewing sounds as the lizard gobbled up its meal. It sounded like someone chewing gum.

"Hungry little dude," I murmured.

The ant disappeared in less than three seconds. The lizard started walking again, in a straight line. It picked up speed. Its head swept from side to side. I realized it must be searching for more ants.

I knew my dad had a big bag of dead crickets waiting, for its meals. I couldn't go get the bag. I couldn't let this creature out of my sight. It was headed toward the open door to the hall.

I couldn't just stare at it any longer. I had to act.

I was still down on my knees. The little hairball turned and disappeared around the side of a cabinet.

*No!*

If I lost it, I'd never forgive myself.

I jumped to my feet and hurtled to the end of the cabinet. My eyes frantically scanned the floor. I didn't see it.

Wait.

*Yes.* There it was. Trotting toward the open door.

*I'll pick it up and put it in the warmer,* I decided. The warmer had a lid on it. So the creature couldn't climb out.

I took a deep breath. Bent down. Reached my open hand to the floor and—

"OUCH!"

It bit me.

# 15

The pain still throbbing, I shook my finger. I examined it. I saw a thin cut, like a small paper cut. A single drop of blood appeared.

I shook the hand again, waiting for the pain to fade. Then I reached down to the floor with my other hand and gently wrapped my fingers around the hairy little creature.

He buzzed and shook his body against my palm. The prickly hair tickled my skin. I hurried to the warmer, hoping the little guy wouldn't bite me again. I breathed a sigh of relief as I lowered him into the warmer. Then I carefully closed the lid and rushed to find my dad.

"Does it still hurt?" Dad asked.

"A little," I said. "Not as bad as before."

Of course, Dad was *dying* to see the lizard. But he decided he should take care of my finger first.

Freddy watched as Dad dabbed the droplets of blood with a cloth. Then he smoothed some ointment over the cut and wrapped a bandage around the finger.

"You're going to get rabies," Freddy said. "Then you're going to froth at the mouth and howl like a dog." He did some ridiculous dog howls.

He thinks he's hilarious. But what's funny about rabies?

"Lizards don't carry rabies," Dad said.

"Just saying," Freddy replied. That didn't make any sense at all.

"Okay. You're all patched up, Kate. Let's go see this guy!" Dad exclaimed. He took off running full speed down the hall.

Freddy and I followed. "Can I hold him?" Freddy called.

"He'll bite you, too," I said. "What makes you think *you're* safe from a lizard bite?"

Freddy raised both hands and grinned at me. He was wearing gloves.

A few seconds later, all three of us were peering into the warmer. The creature already looked bigger to me. And I saw black hairs all over the bottom of the warmer.

"He'll shed that hair and start to look more like a lizard," Dad said. "I . . . I'm so excited, I can barely speak. You realize, don't you, that this is the only Tasmanian cobra lizard in all of America."

"He looks like a fat bug," Freddy said. "Check out those hairy bug legs."

"Give him time," Dad said. "He'll look more like a lizard every day."

"I don't think he's comfortable in the warmer," I said. "Look. He's pacing back and forth. Maybe we should put him in the sand in the glass case. He'll have more room."

"Maybe he's hungry," Freddy said. "Kate, why don't you put your finger in there and see."

I gave Freddy a shove. "Ha-ha."

"Maybe we *should* move him," Dad replied. "I have to call your mother. She won't believe the lizard has hatched and she missed it."

Mom was visiting her sister in Shaker Heights. She wasn't supposed to come home until the weekend.

Dad snapped a couple of photos with his phone. "Wait till she sees this. It's beyond exciting. We're going to be famous, you know."

It was great to see Dad so excited. He'd been really depressed ever since the mini-horse petting farm had to shut down.

"Let's move the lizard to the sandy case," Dad said. "Freddy, you're wearing gloves. Go ahead. You do it."

Freddy's eyes widened in surprise. "Me? Really?"

"Go ahead," Dad said. "Be very careful. Lift him out with two fingers. Don't squeeze too tight." He motioned to the glass case across from us on the worktable. "Then just lower him down gently."

"No problem," Freddy said. "Are you watching, Kate? Watch how an expert does it."

He reached a gloved hand into the warmer. Wrapped his hand around the lizard. He lifted his hand and held it in front of Dad and me.

Then he took his other hand and smashed it into the glove. A strange grin spread over Freddy's face as he smacked the gloves together and crushed the lizard flat.

# 16

I started to choke. Dad stumbled back against the worktable.

Freddy grinned at us and opened both of his gloved hands.

Empty.

"The lizard is still in the warmer," he said. "I'm learning from you, Dad." He waved his empty gloves in the air and burst out laughing.

Dad just gawked at Freddy with his mouth hanging open.

"You—you jerk!" I cried. "You scared me to death!"

Freddy laughed some more. Then he rubbed his glove down my face. "Dad isn't the only funny guy in the family."

Dad let out a long whoosh of air. "I think that joke will be funny in an hour or two, Freddy," he said. "Once my heart starts beating again."

I shook my head. "I like a good laugh," I said. But—"

I stopped because Freddy was reaching into the warmer again. Dad and I both watched in silence as he carefully lifted the baby lizard out. He held it between two fingers.

The lizard had lost most of its hair. Its skin was a light brown color. Its head turned from side to side as Freddy carried it to the worktable. Freddy lifted it over the glass case and lowered it gently onto the sandy bottom.

All three of us froze and peered through the glass. The little creature didn't move. Just hunched on the sand, its spindly legs splayed, its nubby body resting on the bottom.

"Is it dead?" I asked in a tiny voice. "Why isn't it moving?"

"Getting used to the sandy floor," Dad said.

Finally, the lizard raised itself and took a few hesitant steps.

"I'll get it some dinner," Dad said. He crossed the room to the supply closet. A few seconds later, he dropped a dead cricket onto the sand beside the lizard.

The cricket was twice as tall as the lizard, but the lizard didn't wait. It dove at the long black legs of the cricket, opened its jaws, and began to crunch away. He really went at it. It sounded like someone chopping wood.

"This guy likes to eat!" Dad said.

The lizard chomped noisily. He cracked and crunched and devoured two legs. Then he plunged his head into the insect's body and began to chew even louder.

My finger throbbed under the bandage. I suddenly wondered what the lizard would be like when he was older and bigger. Would he be as mean as a crocodile and trap his food between giant, jagged teeth?

Dad gets carried away sometimes. He doesn't always think things through. Had he given any thought to what this full-grown lizard would be like? Had he given any thoughts to safety precautions?

Dad snapped photo after photo of the tiny lizard as it devoured the big, crunchy cricket.

"I'm taking video now," he said. "This guy is going to be famous. And he's going to make us famous." Dad turned to me. "Did I already say that? I'm so excited right now, I don't remember what I've said and what I haven't."

A few minutes later, the lizard stopped eating. It turned and hobbled to the back wall of the case and hunched down. Its body churned and pulsed, as if it was digesting its meal. One cricket leg lay in the sand, all that was left of the big insect.

"That reminds me—*I'm* hungry, too!" Freddy said. "Dad, you do know it's dinnertime, don't you?"

Dad shook his head. "I've lost all track of time."

I started toward the supply closet. "Freddy, how many crickets would you like? Would you like fries with them?"

"You're not funny," Freddy said. "I'm the funny one. Did you forget?"

"Funny looking," I muttered.

"Let's go out and get dinner," Dad said. "How about a bucket of fried chicken? Do you want extra crispy?"

I shuddered. "No way. It would make me think of that poor cricket in there."

So . . . we drove to Chicken Heaven and shared a bucket of chicken and a bunch of sides. And it was awesome, as always. We only went to Chicken Heaven when Mom was away.

And guess what we talked about the whole time?

That's right. The Tasmanian cobra lizard. We spent a lot of time trying to think of a good name for him. I wanted to call it Liz. Short for lizard, get it? We didn't really know if it was male or female.

But Freddy insisted we call it Tas. And Dad thought that was a good, simple, easy-to-remember name. Tas.

And we had a good time, especially since Dad was so happy. And I was happy, too—until we were just about to leave. And I looked at the back of my hands. And they were weird. I mean, the skin was definitely weird.

The backs of my hands had crisscross lines on them. Like cracks in the skin. Only in a pattern. The lines formed diamond shapes on the backs of both hands.

"Dad—" I cried. "Look. The backs of my hands . . . The skin is all cracked. What's going on?"

# 17

Freddy laughed. "You're turning into an old lady."

I raised a fist. "Do you want to live to be an old man? Give me a break."

I shoved my hands under Dad's nose. He grabbed them and examined the backs one by one. He rubbed the back of my right hand with his pointer finger.

"Dry skin," he said. "When we get home, borrow some of your mom's hand lotion from the cabinet in her bathroom."

Only dry skin. I felt a lot better.

I love using all the different lotions Mom has. I couldn't wait to get home.

But I didn't get there right away. As we were driving home from Chicken Heaven, a text popped up on my phone. It was from Adele: *Where are you? Did you forget?*

"Oh, wow," I murmured. "I *did* forget."

"What's wrong?" Dad asked, glancing at me in the rearview mirror.

"I'm supposed to be at school," I said. "A bunch of us are building the set for the school play. I don't *believe* I forgot all about it. I was supposed to be there at seven thirty."

"They can probably get along really well without you," Freddy said. Then he giggled. I was seriously getting tired of his sarcastic sense of humor. What a brat.

"I can drop you at school," Dad said, slowing for a stop sign.

"Okay. Great," I said. "I really can't believe I forgot."

The backs of my hands itched. I scratched them, but it didn't help.

A few minutes later, I rushed into the gym at school. All the lights were on. A group of kids were down on their hands and knees painting an enormous backdrop. It was a Western scene. A blue sky over the desert, with yellow sand, dotted by big cactus plants.

The drama club was going to perform a play called *Superheroes of the West*. It was an original musical play by Mr. Coatley, our drama teacher.

"Sorry I'm late, guys," I called. I dropped down beside Adele and picked up a paintbrush.

"Where were you? Hatching more eggs?" she asked. "Did you bring any lizards with you?"

Some kids laughed.

"You went home too early," I told Adele. "You

missed it. There was a lizard in that broken egg. It came out. It's alive!"

Adele sneered. "Don't make up stories, Kate. I was there, remember? I saw the egg hit the floor. Nothing but yucky green egg yolk."

"I need a bigger brush," a boy named DeWayne Harris said. He was at the very top of the backdrop, painting the sky. "Or maybe a roller. There's too much sky. We're going to be here all night."

DeWayne had blue paint on both of his hands. And a smear of it on his T-shirt.

"Think we should put some clouds up there?" a girl named Alicia Wax asked. "It looks kind of weird just solid like that."

"Haven't you ever heard of a blue sky?" DeWayne asked her.

"Clouds are too hard to draw," a boy named Ethan Sadowski said. "They'll look like white patches we forgot to fill in."

"I have proof that the lizard hatched," I told Adele. I dropped the paintbrush and took out my phone. I found the first photos I'd taken of Tas, and I held them up to her.

Adele squinted at the screen. Then she burst out laughing. "That's not a lizard. That's a dead bumblebee."

"Let me see," Ethan said, grabbing the phone from my hand. He stared at it. "Did your cat cough up a hairball?"

Everyone laughed. They passed the photo from person to person. Everyone agreed it didn't look like a newly hatched lizard.

"You're wrong. It's a very rare lizard," I told them. "That's what it looked like when it came out of the egg. But it's already losing all that thick hair."

Adele sniffed. "Your dad is so weird. I couldn't believe that horrible joke he played on us. How do you know the lizard isn't another one of his jokes?"

"It's too important to him to joke about," I said. "You should see how happy he is."

Adele was staring at my bandaged finger. "What happened to your finger?"

"Nothing," I said. "Just a paper cut." *No way* I was going to tell her the lizard had bitten me. Adele would just sneer and say it looked like a bug bite to her.

We went to work. Adele used a wide brush to paint the sand. I pulled a can of green paint over and began to fill in one of the cactuses.

Down on our hands and knees, we all worked in silence for a while. The only sound was the swoosh and scrape of the paintbrushes against the huge canvas.

After a while, I felt sweat drip down the sides of my face. "Hot in here," I murmured.

I had a sleeveless T-shirt under my long-sleeved top. I raised myself to my knees and pulled the top over my head. I tossed it behind me, rearranged the straps on the sleeveless T, and turned to go back to my cactuses.

I stopped when I saw Adele staring at me.

"What's wrong?" I said.

"Kate, your arms!" she exclaimed. "Did you get tattooed or something?"

The others all stopped working and turned their gaze on me.

I frowned at Adele. "Huh? What are you talking about?"

"Did you paint those on?" Alicia asked.

I lowered my eyes to my arms. And gasped. The tiny lines on my hands ... The lines that formed strange diamond patterns ...

They went all the way up both arms.

# 18

"It's just dry skin," I told everyone. "I have very dry skin."

I pulled the long-sleeved top back on. I didn't want them staring at my arms the rest of the night.

At home, I hurried to my mother's bathroom and found her jars and tubes of moisturizing cream. For the next few days, I practically bathed in the skin lotion. I smoothed it up and down both arms in the morning and after dinner.

I wished Mom would get home from Shaker Heights and help me with this skin problem. I kept checking the mirror, and it didn't seem to be getting any better. The slender lines up and down my arms were not disappearing.

I wanted to tell Dad about it. But he was so busy with the lizard and so tense about the press conference he had set up to tell the world about the lizard, I decided not to bother him with it.

On Sunday, news reporters showed up just before noon. Dad kept them in the living room till everyone had arrived. They had to wait for a TV news crew to arrive.

I counted at least a dozen reporters and almost as many photographers. Dad was right. Having a Tasmanian cobra lizard in Middle Village was really big news.

Mom was due home that afternoon. I felt bad that she had to miss the news conference. She would have enjoyed all the excitement. I had talked to her two or three times on FaceTime, and she was just as excited about the lizard as Dad was.

I helped pass out Cokes and iced tea to the reporters and photographers. Meanwhile, Freddy was going around the room telling them all that he had named the lizard.

When he told them the name was Tas, they all looked disappointed. I mean, it wasn't a very clever name. What was Freddy thinking?

After the reporters and TV crews had all arrived, Dad led them down the hall to the lizard room.

Of course, as soon as they entered, Screech became a macaw maniac. He made such deafening squawks and cries, Dad had to put him in his cage and cover it up. "Afraid he wants to be the star," Dad told everyone.

"Beautiful bird," one of the reporters said. "Aren't you afraid he'll try to eat the lizard?"

Dad stared blankly at the reporter. I could see that Dad had never even thought about that.

He led them all to where he had set up a specially built glass tank to show off the lizard. The tank was six feet long and covered most of the top of the worktable.

The bottom of the tank was covered in green, leafy plants over a layer of sand. A big water bowl stood at the far end.

The reporters began to ooh and ahh as soon as they saw Tas. The TV people eagerly began to set up their lights and ready their cameras.

Tas stood in the middle of the tank, looking out. He had grown a lot. He was about the size of a hamster now, and his skin was different. It was green and bumpy, and with his slender smooth legs and lump of a head, he didn't look like a bug anymore. He looked a lot like a lizard.

His tiny black eyes had grown into wide yellow eyes. He had a purple tongue that he flicked in the air. And a few pointed teeth were poking through the gums in his jaws.

I stood back as one of the TV reporters raised a microphone and prepared to interview my dad. She brushed back her blond hair and cleared her throat. "Ready when you are," she told Dad.

"Do I get to be on TV?" Freddy asked her. "I'm the one who named him."

"Maybe later," she told Freddy. She motioned for him to back away.

In the glass case, Tas strode to the far end and began to chew on a dead cricket. Cameras clicked. Someone whispered: "Mmmmm. That looks tasty."

"Can you tell us how big the lizard will grow?" the TV reporter asked Dad.

"I think he'll be pretty big," Dad replied. "Probably three to four feet long. He should weigh at least seventy or eighty pounds."

"And does he eat only flies and crickets and other insects?"

Dad nodded. "He's a carnivore. A meat eater. But at this small size, I feel that insects are the most meat he can handle."

The reporter asked Dad another question, but I didn't hear it. I felt a strong breeze. And I heard a soft buzzing sound outside the room.

I stepped into the hall and saw two flies buzzing around each other. I felt another strong brush of wind.

I turned and made my way toward the front of the house. I was nearly to the living room when I saw the problem. The reporters had left the front door wide open.

It was a sunny spring day, but very windy. I hurried to the door and pushed it closed. Then I turned back toward the hall and started to return to the news conference.

I stopped when I saw that more flies had come in through the open door. I saw a couple of fat

71

black flies buzzing around on the mirror over the mantelpiece.

Holding my breath, I crept up to them. I shot my hand out and caught them both. Then I stuffed them eagerly into my mouth and chewed them up.

# 19

"Kate—what did you just do?" a voice cried.

I spun away from the mirror and saw Freddy standing right in front of me, his face wide with confusion.

My breath caught in my throat. *He saw me.*

"Kate—" he started. He pointed at the mirror.

My mind whirred.

I forced myself to laugh. "Ha-ha. Did I fool you?"

He blinked. "Huh? Fool me?"

"You're not the only joker in this family," I said. I pressed my hands against my waist. "Did you really think I ate those flies?"

"Well . . . yes," he said.

I laughed again. "I saw you standing there," I lied. "I only did that to gross you out."

"That's sick," he said. He shoved me back against the mantel.

"Just a joke," I said. Meanwhile, the words

repeated in my head: *Kate, what did you just do? Kate, did you really eat two flies?*

"We're missing the news conference," Freddy said. He grinned. "I'm going to be on TV."

"It's not about you," I said. "It's about the lizard. *Everything* isn't about you."

He stuck his tongue out at me and took off, running down the hall back to the lizard room.

I took a deep breath. I felt strange. A little dizzy, maybe. I could hear the voices from down the hall.

A fat fly buzzed over the back of the couch.

I glanced around the living room. No one around now.

I checked down the hall. No one out there. No one watching.

I dove for the fly, snapped my hand around it, and stuffed it into my mouth.

*Three flies. I just ate three flies.*

I started to groan—but stopped when I spotted something moving at the foot of the couch.

I crouched down and saw it. A tiny mouse.

Could I catch it?

My stomach growled.

*No. No, Kate. No.*

I decided to save it for later.

# 20

I knew I had a problem. It's not like my brain wasn't working. I was still me. I was still Kate Lipton, and I knew I had a big, horrifying problem.

I could still taste the flies on my tongue. They tasted kind of metallic. A little bit bitter, but not too bad.

*I ate flies.*

*I ate flies and I liked them.*

I had to tell Dad. Mom wouldn't be home for hours. I needed help desperately, right now.

But what could I do? The house was full of reporters and cameras and TV interviewers.

I couldn't burst in and say, "Dad, I have a problem. My skin is turning all lined and bumpy. And I caught some flies and ate them. And I saw a mouse, and it made me hungry."

I stood there in the middle of the living room. The room was spinning. The whole house was spinning around me, whirling around like my crazy thoughts.

I could hear laughter from down the hall in the lizard room. A man was asking my dad more questions.

I couldn't go back in there. I felt too weird. I was afraid of what I might say or do. I didn't want to upset my dad in any way. This was his big day. His day to show the rare, precious lizard to the world and announce his big plans for a lizard attraction in Middle Village.

He was so proud and happy. I couldn't spoil it for him. My problem would have to wait.

I staggered into the hall. I shook my head hard, trying to stop everything from spinning. I made my way to the stairs. I didn't really know where I was going. To my room?

Yes. I climbed the stairs and walked down the hall to my room. And before I realized it, I was taking off my clothes. And stepping into my bathroom shower.

Yes. A shower. A long, hot shower. Without thinking about it, I realized that's what I needed. I needed hot water to wash away all the weirdness. To wash all the dryness from my skin. A long shower to sweep away all my scary thoughts and hungers.

The hot water drummed against my body. I shut my eyes and let the water carry me away, soothe me, relax me, make me feel like myself again.

Steam rose around me. I wanted to hide inside it. Let it curl around me and close me inside, where I'd be safe.

I don't know how long I stood there. When I shut off the water and stepped out of the shower, the bathroom was completely fogged up.

I moved to the mirror. Coated with steam. I grabbed a towel and wiped off the glass, wiped it till I could see clearly.

And I let out a cry.

The crisscross skin lines covered my shoulders now. My arms . . . my shoulders. The strange patterns in my skin—were spreading all over me.

The shower hadn't helped at all. I knew what was happening. It was too horrifying to put into words. But I knew . . .

I suddenly remembered something. It flashed into my mind. I could picture it so clearly.

I pulled my bathrobe around me and tightened the belt. Then I walked back into my room and crossed to the dresser.

*I think it's in the bottom dresser drawer.*

That's where I dump all the things I want to keep but I know I'll never use.

I slid open the drawer. It was jammed with old T-shirts, and vests, and sweatpants, and junk jewelry in a red wooden box, and some other boxes I didn't know what they contained . . . and . . . yes. The little purse.

I tugged the little purse out from beneath a tangle of silvery belts. I had to untangle the knotted strap. Then I gave a hard tug and the purse came out.

I stared at it. The little yellow-brown purse my grandmother gave me a few years ago. I smoothed my fingers over the side. Like smooth leather but with lined patterns. Slender lines crisscrossing everywhere.

Just like my skin. The same pattern. The same.

My hands trembled as I opened the little purse. I found the tag inside and held it close to my face to read it.

*Yes. Yes. I knew it.*

The purse was made from lizard skin.

# 21

I gripped the little bag in my trembling hands. I rubbed my fingers over the lizard skin. Then I swept my right hand down my left arm.

*My lizard skin arm.*

That tiny lizard bit me, and now my skin was changing, and I was eating flies. Eating flies and enjoying them. I was turning into a lizard.

I had to tell Dad. But what could he do? He wasn't a scientist or a doctor. He just had a crazy idea to start a lizard collection.

"He'll take me to Dr. Wilkinson," I said out loud. "Dr. Wilkinson will know how to help me."

My heart was beating like crazy. I tossed the little purse onto my bed. Then I pulled on jeans and a sweatshirt and hurried downstairs.

"Dad! Where are you?" I shouted. "I have to tell you something. Dad?"

I ran through the living room toward the back hall. The reporters had all left. The house was silent. The only sounds I heard were the steady ticking of the grandfather clock beside the mantel and the pounding of my bare feet on the floorboards.

"Dad? Where are you?"

I had to show him my lizard skin. I had to tell him about the flies I ate. With each step, I became more frantic. I started to choke. It felt as if my heart had jumped into my throat.

"Dad?"

I peered into the kitchen. No sign of him. *He must still be in the lizard room,* I realized.

I turned and ran down the hall. The door was shut. I could hear the macaw squawking inside the room. No other voices.

I grabbed the handle and tugged the door open. "Dad?"

I screamed when I saw the giant creature hunched over the worktable. A scaly green lizard. At least six feet tall. The creature stood balanced on its two hind legs and its fat tail.

It turned slowly at the sound of my voice. It lowered its warty head and stared. It saw me. It saw me and it flicked a long purple tongue at me.

And I screamed again.

# 22

The huge lizard flicked its long tongue at me again and again.

I spun away. I tried to run, but in my panic, I stumbled into the door. I grabbed the edge of the door to hold myself up.

Panting like an animal, I glanced back—and saw the lizard take a heavy step toward me.

"Nooooo!" My scream rang down the hall.

I stumbled again. Caught my balance. And bolted away, my bare feet slapping the floor.

"Dad! Where are you? Dad?" I screamed breathlessly.

Was he upstairs in his room? Had he gone out with some of the reporters? No. He wouldn't have left without telling Freddy and me.

I grabbed the banister and pulled myself up the stairs. The door to his bedroom was open. I burst inside. "Dad?"

No sign of him. The bed was made. Some

shirts had been tossed onto the chair beside the bed.

I took a deep, shuddering breath. I returned to the stairs. I peered down over the banister. No sign of the enormous lizard. Was he waiting for me somewhere? Hiding behind the couch? Waiting to pounce?

Then I spotted Dad by the front door. He was dressed in a business suit. He dropped a suitcase by the door.

"Dad!" I shouted. I hurtled down the stairs.

"Kate, I was looking for you," he said. "I have to leave. Something wonderful just came up, and I have to go right now."

"Dad—listen to me!" I cried. "A lizard, Dad. A giant lizard!" I pointed frantically toward the lizard room down the hall.

His face twisted in alarm. He grabbed my shoulders. "Easy. Take a breath. Easy. You're shaking!"

"Listen to me," I insisted. "There's a giant lizard in the house. I mean *giant*. In the lizard room. Quick!"

Dad held on to me. "Wait. Wait. I was in the lizard room just a little while ago. I didn't see any giant lizard."

"Don't just stand there!" I screamed. I tugged free, spun away from him, and took off. "Come on! Hurry!" I shouted.

I raced back down the hall to the lizard room.

I knew I had left the door open when I turned and ran from the monster lizard. But the door was shut now.

Dad caught up to me. He squinted hard at me, as if he was trying to decide whether I was crazy or not. Then he pulled open the door and we both peered into the room.

"There it is!" I shouted.

# 23

But I wasn't staring at a giant lizard. I was staring at a large green trash bag folded over the top of the worktable.

Dad didn't say a word, but his eyes were still studying me. We stepped into the room. "Looks like a trash bag to me," Dad murmured.

"But—But—" I sputtered.

The macaw hopped up and down excitedly on his perch. The Tasmanian cobra lizard sat at one end of his long glass case. His head was raised but his eyes were shut. As we stepped near, he remained very still. Asleep on his feet.

"I . . . I'm not crazy," I stammered. "I didn't see a trash bag. It was a huge lizard standing on two feet, and it started to come after me."

Dad turned and glanced all around the room. "No place for a giant lizard to hide," he said. "Kate, do you think maybe your imagination . . ." His voice trailed off. He eyed the trash bag.

"I don't know what to think," I confessed. "I . . . I really don't."

I followed him back to the living room. "Dad, what's up with the suitcase?"

"I told you, something very exciting has come up. And I have to make a fast trip to Toronto."

My mouth dropped open. "Huh? Toronto?"

He nodded. "They have a lizard for us. It just arrived. It's being held by customs up there. I have to show the papers so I can bring it home."

"But, Dad—" I started.

"Mrs. Overman is coming to stay with you and Freddy. I'm really sorry I have to leave before your mother gets home. But your aunt Bethany is sick. So Mom is staying a few more days in Shaker Heights."

I groaned. "Ohhh no. Not Mrs. Overman. She just sits and knits all day, and falls asleep with her mouth wide open and makes sounds like a bullfrog."

"That's good," Dad said. "Then she won't be in your way." He glanced out the front window. "There's my cab."

He started to lift his suitcase, but I grabbed his arm. "Dad, I have to talk to you. My skin—"

In the driveway, the taxi driver honked his horn.

"I'm sure Mrs. Overman can help you with skin problems," Dad said. He kissed my forehead.

"Dad, it's important!" I cried.

"Text me, okay?" he replied. The taxi honked again. "I'm very late. Text me, Kate. I'll try to call from Toronto."

Then he was out the door. I watched him run to the taxi.

"Did Dad leave?" Freddy called. He was half-way down the stairs.

"Yes. He had a taxi waiting," I said.

Freddy's face drooped. "He forgot to say good-bye."

"He had to hurry to Toronto," I explained. "He said there's a lizard waiting for him there."

Freddy nodded. Then he narrowed his eyes at me. "Hey, how did you do that to your finger-nails? Awesome!"

"Huh?" I raised both hands and squinted at the nails. My fingernails had all changed shape. They came to sharp points now. Like lizard toenails.

# 24

"Grrrrr." I growled at Freddy and swept my hands up and down, pretending to claw him. "The nails come in a kit," I lied. "Awesome, right?"

"Awesome," he said. He turned to go back to his room.

"Wait. Freddy, don't go," I said.

He spun back. "I'm in the middle of a game."

"Save it," I said. I stepped closer to him. "Listen to me. We're not safe here."

He grinned. "I get it. Dad left, so you're trying to scare me?"

I shook my head. "No. Listen. I'm serious. I saw something. In the hatching room. I swear. It was a huge lizard. At least six feet tall. It was standing on its rear legs. It turned and saw me."

Freddy laughed. "No way, Kate. I'm not buying it. Do you think I'm stupid or something?"

I pounded the banister with my fist. "I'm serious!" I shouted. "I'm not joking. There's a creature somewhere in this house. We're not safe here."

I took another step toward him. "Stop laughing, Freddy. It isn't a joke. If you don't stop laughing, you'll be sorry!"

His grin faded. He studied my face. I could see he was thinking hard. "A six-foot-tall lizard?" he said finally. "Was its name Godzilla?" He burst out laughing again.

I wanted to strangle him. Instead, I spun away from him, clenching my fists at my sides.

"You know it had to be Dad," Freddy said. "Dad and his jokes. He was probably trying on a new Halloween costume."

I turned and frowned at him. "It's May. It's nowhere near Halloween."

"That wouldn't stop Dad," he shot back.

I ignored that. "Dad believed me," I said. That wasn't exactly true. But I was desperate.

"Is that why he left?" Freddy said.

"Come on. Help me find it," I said. "It could be hiding anywhere. There are so many empty rooms in this old house. Come search with me, okay?"

He shook his head. "I don't think so." He turned and started back up the stairs. "Good luck with it."

The little punk. "I hope the lizard *eats* you!" I shouted. "You *insect*!"

Of course he laughed.

I knew the giant lizard was hiding somewhere. I knew I hadn't imagined it.

I began my search in the hatching room. Had the creature returned to where I had seen it? No. Screech was asleep on his perch. The Tasmanian cobra lizard was also asleep, flat on its stomach in its case. No sign of any intruder.

My throat was dry and my stomach felt tight with dread. I didn't really want to find the giant lizard. What would I do if I found it?

But I had to know if it was lurking somewhere. Waiting until after dark, maybe, so it could sneak up on us. Waiting to pounce. Waiting to devour Freddy and me.

I forced myself to explore the back hall. This was the part of the house that we didn't use. Some of the rooms had cartons stacked up in them and old furniture covered with sheets. Other rooms were empty and coated with thick layers of dust.

I used my phone as a flashlight to peer into the empty rooms. Most of them didn't have light. The old floorboards creaked under my feet.

I was alert to every sound. Every creak, every crack, every thump made my heart skip a beat. I moved quickly from room to room, sweeping the white light around, squinting hard, searching for anything that moved.

I cried out when two mice scampered right over my feet and darted into an empty bedroom.

I nearly dropped the phone. By the time I reached the end of the hall, my teeth were chattering.

"Hey, Lizard—where are you?" I called, my voice trembling in the dusty air.

I started to return to the front of the house. But I stopped with a sharp gasp as I heard a noise up ahead. I held my breath. And listened.

And heard a soft thud. A floorboard creak. And then another thud and a scraping sound.

My whole body shuddered. Footsteps. Soft footsteps from the end of the hall.

*I've found it,* I realized.

I knew I'd find the huge, ugly creature. I was desperate to find it. To prove I hadn't imagined it. But now I just wanted to hide from it. My legs trembled. I tried to force my body to tense itself. I prepared to run.

More footsteps. More creaks and groans.

Then, before I could move, it loomed out of the shadows—and I started to scream.

# 25

"Kate! There you are!" a voice called.

Trembling, I gaped at the large creature.

No. Not a creature. Not a creature at all.

A large, white-haired woman in a baggy gray sweatsuit.

"Mrs. Overman?" I choked out in a high, shrill voice. "I—"

"I thought I heard you," she said. "What are you doing back here? Why were you screaming?"

"Uh . . . it was nothing. I was just looking for something, and some mice scared me," I stammered. With a relieved sigh, I made my way down the hall to her.

When she smiled, a hundred little wrinkles formed around her eyes. It suddenly reminded me of lizard skin. "I let myself in," she said. "But I couldn't find you or your brother."

"Freddy is upstairs in his room," I said. I began to lead the way to the kitchen. "How are you, Mrs. Overman?"

She sighed. "Hanging in. Your dad called me at the last minute. I'm glad I had no plans."

"Me too," I said. "He had to go pick up a lizard in Toronto."

Her eyes widened in surprise for just a second. "Barry has some crazy ideas sometimes, doesn't he?"

I had to agree, and I laughed. But then I pictured the six-foot-tall lizard, standing at the worktable in the hatching room. And I shivered.

I stared at the lizard skin on my hands, my arms. My curled nails.

How would I sleep tonight? How would I ever sleep again?

I tossed and turned all night. Every time I started to drift off, a noise or a gust of wind blowing my bedroom curtains or a squeak or a moan of the creaky old house shocked me alert again.

A beam of silvery moonlight poured over my bed from the window and lighted my cracked lizard skin. I forced back the urge to burst into sobs.

How could I go to school looking like this? How could I keep the other kids from seeing that I was turning into a freak of nature? What if I ate the class hamster or gobbled down insects in front of everyone?

But then I remembered that today was Ms.

Arnold's science test. And I had promised to help finish the set for the play. And oral book reports in the afternoon.

I couldn't stay home. I wanted to hide. Hide forever. But I had to go. I pulled on a long-sleeved shirt to cover my lizard arms.

It was a hot day. The sun was beaming down in a clear blue sky. I was sweating by the time I walked the three blocks to school.

I stepped into Ms. Arnold's class with my hands in my jeans pockets. With my pointed nails and lined and wrinkled skin, I looked like I had stepped out of a horror movie.

I slumped into my seat. Luckily, it was in the back row of the room.

Sunlight washed over me from the open window. The sun warmed my skin. I turned to the window and shut my eyes. I pictured myself slithering out the window and lying on my stomach in the grass. Basking in the sun. Letting the sun warm my back. I wanted to sun myself for hours.

I felt a hand on my sleeve. I jumped, suddenly alert. I turned to see Adele staring at me. Adele sits next to me in almost every class. She really thinks she's my friend. Or maybe she thinks that makes it easier to compete with me in everything we do.

She pinched my shirtsleeve between her fingers. "Long sleeves on such a hot day?"

I nodded. "My mom has been away. No one did any laundry. It was the only thing in my drawer."

"She's been gone a long time," Adele whispered. "Did your parents break up or something?"

"No way," I shot back. Adele always tried to stir up gossip. She's a real troublemaker.

"Kate, could I have your attention?" Ms. Arnold called from the front of the room.

Kids turned to stare at me. I could feel my face turning hot, and I knew I was blushing. "Sorry," I muttered.

Ms. Arnold dropped onto the edge of her desk, bumping her coffee cup. She caught the cup as it started to fall and placed it back on the desktop.

"Good catch!" Ira Forrest yelled, and everyone clapped.

Ms. Arnold smiled. "Everyone is in such a good mood this morning," she said. "I guess it's because of all the sunshine."

*I'm not in a good mood*, I thought. *I'm scared and tense, and I just keep wondering what's going to happen to me next? And who can help me?*

"Adele had a very good idea that I want to share with you," Ms. Arnold said. "Actually, Adele, why don't you tell us about it?"

"Okay," Adele agreed. She jumped to her feet. She swept back her hair with one hand. "Here's my idea. I think we should all bring in baby pictures. We can make an Instagram album. See? We upload photos of what we look like now and put them next to what we looked like as babies."

No one said anything. Adele looked disappointed. What did she expect? Did she think we'd all burst into applause at that idea? She dropped back onto her chair.

"I love this idea," Ms. Arnold said. "I think it could be very funny. Get your parents to help you find a baby photo or two that we can use. It will make a great class album."

Ms. Arnold took a long sip of coffee. "And thank you, Adele, for such a terrific idea."

Adele took a short bow in her seat. She had a big smile on her face. She loves scoring points with the teacher. She turned to me with a look of triumph on her face.

I could read her thoughts: *I win, Kate. Score one for me.*

No big deal. My day was about to get a lot worse.

"Okay, everyone," Ms. Arnold said. "You're dismissed. Go get changed for gym class."

# 26

Oh no. Gym class. If I changed into my gym shorts and T-shirt, everyone would see what was happening to me.

No. No way. No way.

The other kids all hurried to the locker rooms to get changed. I lingered in the gym till Ms. Baylor, the Phys Ed teacher, showed up.

She began sliding the volleyball nets into place. I crossed the gym to talk to her.

Ms. Baylor doesn't look like the standard gym teacher. She's small, very petite. She has long black hair that she wears in a single braid. She's real pretty, with high cheekbones and big brown eyes.

"Ms. Baylor, I'm so sorry," I said. "I took my gym clothes home to wash them, and I forgot to bring them back."

She shrugged her slender shoulders. She seemed so tiny in her maroon sweatsuit. "No problem, Kate," she said. "We're playing volleyball this morning. You're wearing sneakers, right? So why don't you play in your street clothes?"

I felt so relieved, I wanted to hug her.

A few minutes later, the rest of the class came trotting out, ready to play. Adele came running up to me. She had her hair tied back with a blue hairband. She wore a pale blue sleeveless T-shirt tucked into white tennis shorts.

Of course, she had to question me. "Why aren't you dressed?"

I repeated my lie. "I took my stuff home to be washed and forgot to bring it back."

She sneered. "You're weird, Kate. Whoever heard of washing your gym clothes?" She turned and shouted to a bunch of other kids. "Hey, did you know Kate is a clean freak?"

*I'm just a freak*, I thought bitterly. I had my hands curled tightly. I hoped no one could see my pointed nails.

*A freak. A freak. A freak.*

The game went pretty well. I tried to stay back, away from where the ball was being hit. Adele kept jumping in front of me, hitting balls that I should have had. But I didn't care. She could be the star today. How could I even think about a volleyball game when I was turning into a lizard?

I breathed a sigh of relief when Ms. Baylor blew the whistle ending the game. I watched everyone jog to the locker rooms to shower and change back into their clothes.

*I made it through the game. And no one saw my skin or claws.*

I felt good for only a few seconds. Then the trouble started.

Ms. Baylor deposited the volleyball back in the supply closet. Then she gave me a wave. "Don't forget your gym clothes next time, Kate," she called. She disappeared out of the gym.

I stood there all alone. Sunlight poured in from the high windows all around. The shiny gym floor reflected the bright light.

Suddenly, I had a strange feeling sweep down over me. I shuddered. My skin tingled.

I lowered myself to my knees. I brought my hands down in front of me.

*What am I doing?*

*Kate, stop. Stop. Don't do this.*

But I couldn't control myself. Slowly, I began crawling on all fours across the gym floor.

# 27

As I crawled, I moved my head from side to side. I flicked my tongue out. Was that my tongue? It seemed longer. Darker.

The floor felt warm under my hands. I raised my head to the windows and let the bright sunlight wash over me. I shut my eyes and enjoyed the feeling as it spread over my back.

Then I crawled some more, moving slowly, enjoying the warmth from the windows above. Near the wall, I spotted something small and dark on the shiny gym floor.

I crawled closer and saw that it was a bug—a beetle, I think. It was on its back, its tiny legs all moving frantically, helplessly trying to turn itself over.

I watched the fat insect struggle. Then I flipped my tongue out, caught it, and snapped it into my mouth. It had a sour taste, and I could feel the little legs brush the top of my mouth as I started to chew it.

It made a crunching sound as I bit through its shell. I swallowed it, the sour taste lingering on my tongue. It went down easily. I lowered my head and moved it from side to side, searching for more.

I turned and started to crawl toward the gym doors.

*I've got to stand up. I have to walk. Fight this crazy urge.*

My mind whirred as my human self battled to take charge. I had to get control.

*Stand up, Kate. Climb to your feet. You can do it. Stand up.*

But my body wouldn't cooperate. My legs refused to pull me up. I flicked my tongue out and slowly ... slowly ... like a big lizard ... crawled toward the exit.

And that's when I saw Adele.

She was back in her regular clothes. She had her phone raised in front of her. "I'm getting this on video," she said. "Keep crawling. This is hilarious. Wait till everyone sees it."

# 28

I froze. I hunched there on my hands and knees, my head low, my tongue out.

I stared up at Adele. Watched her ugly laughter. Saw her holding the phone up, the lens aimed down at me.

And suddenly, she turned red. The gym turned red. Everything became a blinding red in my eyes.

I snapped my jaws. I suddenly had one thought in my mind: *Hurt her.*

I turned. I was down so low, my stomach rubbed the gym floor.

Adele had her phone aimed at me. "Keep moving!" she shouted. "I'm loving this."

*Not for long,* I thought.

I crawled toward her, slow at first, then picking up speed. She was a dark form inside a solid red world. Like a black shadow looming over me, surrounded by red . . . by my red anger.

I flicked my tongue at her. I snapped my jaws.

*Hurt her . . . Hurt her . . .*

Adele laughed. "This is priceless! Awesome!"

I knew I had to fight my lizard anger. I struggled to get my control back. I blinked, trying to clear away the red.

But I couldn't stop myself.

*Hurt her. Hurt her.*

A hoarse growl escaped my throat. I snapped my teeth again.

I tensed my legs, preparing to leap onto her.

I saw Adele's expression change. Her smile faded. Her eyes bulged. "Hey!" she cried out, lowering her phone. "Hey—stop! What are you *doing*?"

I crawled closer. I raised myself up rapidly, faster than I could imagine. I jumped to my feet, ready to attack.

"Nooooo!" Adele's scream shocked me to my senses.

We both stood there, breathing hard, gaping at each other, studying each other. We were both asking ourselves the same question: *Did this really happen?*

"I thought you had really lost your mind for a second," she said.

I suddenly felt weary. I uttered a long sigh.

Adele slowly relaxed. She raised the phone and clicked off the video.

"Adele . . ." I choked out, finding my voice, my human voice. "Adele . . . what are you going to do with that video?" I demanded.

"Put it on YouTube, of course," she said. "And on my Facebook page. So everyone will see it."

I stared at her. I wrapped my arms around myself. "But . . . Adele . . ."

Her eyes locked on mine. "Kate, why did you do that? Why were you crawling on the floor like that?"

"Just being silly," I said. "Kind of a workout, you know? Crawling like that is good for the back. I was just working on my back muscles while I was waiting for everyone."

She stared at me without replying. I could see that she didn't believe me.

"Adele," I said, lowering my voice to a whisper. "You're not really going to put that video online, are you?"

She squeezed my wrist. "Hey, I'm your friend, Kate. Would I do a thing like that to a friend?"

# 29

I met Freddy in the playground after school, and we walked home together. I didn't say much. I was too frightened and upset to pretend things were normal.

Freddy was all excited about some Civil War battles that they talked about in his class. He said he wanted to explore farm fields and find some old swords or cannonballs. He said he could collect the Civil War stuff and sell it on eBay for a ton of money.

"I don't want to discourage you," I said. "But I don't think there were any Civil War battles in Middle Village."

"Maybe there were, and I could be the first to find the stuff," he said. He suddenly reminded me a lot of Dad. Crazy schemes.

At home, I went to my room and tried to work on a homework report. But, of course, it was impossible. I stared at myself in my dresser mirror. Was I about to lose myself completely and turn into a lizard forever?

While I gazed in the mirror, trembling, I finally got a text from Dad. He said he was still in Toronto. He was having trouble claiming the lizard. He said he would try to get home as soon as possible, but he'd definitely be home sometime tomorrow, and we could talk.

Tomorrow seemed a long time away.

Would Adele put that video on YouTube? If she did, my life would be over by tomorrow.

But maybe my life would be over anyway. Maybe my lizard life would begin tomorrow and I wouldn't care about YouTube videos.

I decided I had no choice. I had to tell Mrs. Overman my problem. She had to get me to a doctor. Any doctor.

I ran downstairs. "Mrs. Overman? Are you here?"

I saw her knitting piled on the kitchen table. She seemed to be knitting one very long blue sleeve. I guess she starts with the sleeves and then knits the middle of the sweater.

I turned when the kitchen door opened and Mrs. Overman came in, her arms loaded down with grocery bags.

I hurried over to help her. I took one of the heavy bags to the counter.

"I thought I'd make chicken tonight," she said,

fluffing up her curly white hair with both hands. "Is that all right?"

"Nice," I said. "But . . . I have to talk to you."

She nodded. "Okay."

I helped her unpack the bags. She had three packages of raw chicken breasts and legs. She spread them out on the counter.

"Oh, my goodness!" she cried. "I left a whole bag at the store. I have to go back."

"But, Mrs. Overman—" I started.

She was out the door before I could stop her. "Be right back," she called.

Shaking my head, I started for my room. But I stopped at the kitchen counter and gazed at the packages of raw chicken. My stomach gnawed. I hadn't realized how hungry I was.

The raw chicken smelled tangy and sweet. My mouth began to water.

*What am I doing?*

I ripped the covers off the packages. I grabbed a raw chicken breast and stuffed it into my mouth. It was rubbery and kind of slimy. Hard to chew.

But I gobbled down a chicken breast and reached for another.

The juice from the raw meat ran down my chin and spread over my cheeks. I tore off a chunk of leg and chewed it furiously, swallowing with a loud *gulp* and chewing off some more.

I was breathing hard, my chest heaving up and down, my stomach growling. I devoured the chicken leg and tossed the bone onto the counter.

I reached for the other leg. But it slipped from my hand when I heard a loud cry. A shout from right behind me.

I turned to see Freddy in the kitchen doorway. His eyes bulged and his mouth hung open in shock.

*"What are you staring at?"* I snarled in a gruff raspy voice from deep in my throat.

"Kate . . . Kate . . ." he stammered. "You . . . you're acting like an *animal*!"

I let out a roar. I grabbed up the chicken leg and heaved it at him.

Freddy dodged to the side. The leg smacked the wall and slid to the floor.

Roaring like a beast, I pushed myself away from the counter, spread my arms as if preparing to tackle him, and ran. Ran at Freddy.

I grabbed him before he had a chance to move.

He let out a startled squeal as I lowered my head and sank my teeth into the back of his neck.

# 30

"You animal! You animal!" Freddy shrieked.

He tore away from me and pressed a hand to his neck where I had bitten him. He swung his fist wildly. Missed me. Screamed again. And went running from the kitchen.

"Animal! You crazy animal!"

I watched him stumble up the stairs. I heard the door to his room slam.

I stood there in the doorway, breathing hard, holding on to the sides of the doorframe.

I shut my eyes and forced my body to stop shuddering.

*Breathe. Just breathe, Kate.*

The taste of the raw chicken lingered in my mouth. Once again, I pictured myself leaping onto my brother and biting his neck.

*Breathe. Just breathe.*

Slowly, I felt myself return to normal. My stomach had been gnawing and growling and churning. It stopped and now just felt heavy from the chicken parts I'd devoured.

"I have to apologize to Freddy," I said out loud. I started toward his room when my phone rang. I squinted at the screen. Adele. I didn't want to answer. I was in no mood for Adele. But my finger swiped across the screen.

"Kate, I need you to do me a favor," she said.

"A favor?"

"I need you to pick up my two brothers after school tomorrow and take them to their orthodontist appointment."

I pulled the phone from my ear and stared at it for a few seconds. "Excuse me? Why do you need me to do it?"

"Because I don't feel like it," she answered.

"But, Adele—" My voice got shrill. "I don't feel like it, either. I'm not your slave."

"Yes, you are," she said softly. "Did you forget I have that video of you on the gym floor?" She giggled.

"You mean if I don't pick up your brothers . . ." My voice trailed off.

"That's right," she said.

My mouth suddenly felt dry. *I might be a lizard any minute now. And even if I find a way to stop that, I'll be Adele's slave forever.*

I had no choice. "Okay," I replied. "I guess I can do it. I don't really have a choice, do I?"

"No, you don't."

I wished Adele was standing beside me. If she was here, I could bite her in the neck.

She clicked off. I was breathing hard again, seething with anger. I squeezed the phone so hard, my hand ached.

"This is all that stupid lizard's fault," I told myself. "It has ruined my life."

The stupid cobra lizard bit me the day it arrived. And the bite was turning me into a lizard.

I stormed down the hall to the hatching room, swinging my fists. My anger made it hard to breathe. I burst into the room and blinked, waiting for my eyes to adjust to the bright light.

Screech, the big macaw, watched me as I strode to the worktable. He squawked once, then his eyes followed me. He ruffled his feathers. He suddenly seemed very interested in me.

*Does he sense that I'm becoming a lizard?*

*Animals can sense changes.*

*Sometimes it makes them anxious. Nervous.*

The Tasmanian cobra lizard was awake, nibbling on a cricket at the far end of its glass case. It turned its head as I stepped close.

I lowered my head and gazed at it. It stared back with its eerie yellow eyes. I wondered if it could sense the anger I felt.

The lizard flicked its slender purple tongue at me. I flicked my tongue back at it. It tilted its head and stared hard. I did the same.

110

"I hate you!" I screamed. "Do you hear me? I *hate* you!"

And then . . . I can't really explain why I did what I did. My anger just boiled over, and I totally lost it.

# 31

The lid to the glass case was a metal screen. I grabbed it and swung it off the case, and heaved it across the room.

Then I reached down with both hands, grabbed the lizard around its middle, and hoisted it into the air.

The world went red again. Waves of red pulsed in my eyes.

"You're ruining my life!" I shrieked at it. And I started to shake it. I shook it hard, and its head bobbed back and forth.

I screamed out my anger and shook the creature. I lost all control. I was out of my mind. I wanted to destroy it.

Suddenly, it swung its head toward me, snapped its jaws, and bit my wrist.

"Owwwww," I cried out, shocked by the pain as it swept up my arm.

My hand snapped open and I dropped the lizard.

It hit the floor with a loud *plop*. It remained still for only a second or two. Then its legs began to scramble, and it began to run, heading toward the open door.

*Let it go,* I thought bitterly. *Who cares?*

But then I had a serious thought: *The cobra lizard's bite caused my problem. If a doctor can find a cure for me . . . if a doctor can find a way to return me to myself . . . He or she may need to see this lizard. The doctors may need to study it to find the cure.*

*My life may depend on that lizard,* I realized. And there I was, letting it escape.

With a cry, I hurtled myself after it. The lizard ran in a straight line, its four legs clicking on the tile floor.

I took a deep breath and dove for it. My knees hit the floor hard. I reached out both hands and cupped them around the creature's fat middle.

No.

I missed.

The lizard was surprisingly fast. My hands closed around nothing but air. The long tail brushed my hands as the lizard pulled itself out of the room.

I scrambled to the door and watched it scuttle down the hall, picking up speed as it neared the living room.

*I'll never be able to catch it,* I thought.

*What have I done? What have I done?*

# 32

"It can't leave the house," I told myself. "The doors are closed and it can't reach the windows."

I stumbled into the hall. My legs were like rubber. I forced myself to breathe. I'd never felt this kind of panic. It made me want to curl into a tight ball and hide from the world and never move again.

But I had to capture that lizard.

It stepped into a shaft of sunlight as it entered the living room. It moved so rapidly, in a straight line, not swinging its head, not looking to the left or right.

I ran on tiptoes. I wanted to take it by surprise.

The creature was a few feet from the back of the green leather couch. Did it plan to hide under it?

I gasped as it suddenly stopped. I saw its head snap and heard the loud click of its jaws. It pulled something off the floor in its teeth.

I grabbed the sides of the doorway and squinted into the square of sunlight. The lizard tilted its head up. I saw something kicking and thrashing, held in its teeth.

A mouse.

The lizard had caught a mouse. Its jaws were locked around the mouse's middle. The tiny creature squeaked and squealed, kicked its scrawny feet and swung its tail frantically as the lizard tightened its jaws around it.

I let out a long whoosh of air. This might have been the first time I ever felt glad that our house was infested with mice.

I crept closer.

The lizard gave a violent snap of its head. The mouse uttered its final squeak. It slumped in the lizard's mouth. Not moving now. Dead.

The lizard's jaws worked up and down as it began to chew into its prey.

I burst forward. I grabbed the lizard tightly around its middle and lifted it off the floor. Startled, the lizard's eyes bulged. It shot its head from side to side—and dropped the dead mouse.

I raised the lizard high in front of me, gripping it as tightly as I could. It snapped its teeth at me, but I held it too far in front of me. It couldn't reach me.

"You're going back in your case," I told it. "Your vacation is over."

It snapped at me again. Missed.

I took a few steps toward the hall. Then I stopped.

I turned around and gazed down at the floor. My stomach gnawed at me.

That dead mouse looked mighty tempting.

*Maybe I'll just take one bite.*

# 33

I gripped the lizard tightly under one arm and reached for the dead mouse with my other hand. I lifted it by its stub of a tail and dangled it in front of my lips.

My mouth was watering. My stomach growled hungrily.

"Nooooo!" I cried. Fighting it. Fighting the sudden hunger. Fighting the tasty aroma from the mouse's body. "Nooooo!"

I flung the mouse across the room. It bounced against the wall and dropped to the floor. I forced myself to spin away from it.

I trotted back to the hatching room and lowered the lizard into its case. It didn't seem happy to be back. It began pacing from one end of the case to the other, head low, keeping its yellow eyes on me as it walked.

I carefully lowered the screen in place over the top of the case. I let out a long whoosh of air. But I didn't have long to celebrate.

I saw a flash of color dart through the air. Red and blue, like a flame. I didn't have time to duck. Or even scream.

Shrieking angrily, the macaw attacked me. It landed on my head and scraped its talons in my hair. Flapping and shrieking, it bit and scratched.

I cried out in pain as it dug into my hair. I struggled to shove it off.

I ducked and twisted and squirmed. But it kept its grip and kept slashing at me with its pointed beak.

"I'm not a lizard!" I screamed. I must have been insane. Did I expect the bird to understand?

I pressed my arms over my head, trying to protect myself from its vicious attack. Unable to see, I staggered to the worktable.

"Get off! Get off me!"

I sank my hand into the bag of dead crickets. And tossed a handful of the dry, spiny bugs onto the floor.

The macaw squawked. I felt the air from its flapping wings. The talons loosened their grip on my hair.

"Yesss!" I cried as the bird lifted off me and dove for the crickets on the floor.

Gasping for breath, I spun away. I staggered out of the room. Slammed the door hard behind me.

I slapped at my hair with both hands, trying

to push it back into place. My whole head throbbed from the bird's bites and scratches.

"I . . . I need help." I hurtled upstairs to my room. I tried phoning both of my parents. But each call went straight to voice mail.

I texted them. I told them to call me as soon as they could. I said I needed help fast.

I heard music coming from Freddy's room. *I'd better stay away from him,* I thought. *I don't want to scare him more than I already have.*

I sprawled on top of my bed and covered my face with my hands. I wanted to crawl under the covers and never come out.

*Dad wants to open a lizard farm. And his own daughter will be one of the lizards.*

I pictured myself on display. Pacing back and forth on all fours in a cage. Sunning on a rock. Flicking my long tongue at flies. Crowds staring at me. Tossing me insects and popcorn and pieces of lettuce and bread crusts to eat.

I sat up with a shudder.

I knew I couldn't just lie there in bed frightening myself. I had to do something. I had to distract my mind somehow until Mom or Dad returned.

"Oh, wait," I murmured. I suddenly remembered Adele's idea for a project in school. Ms. Arnold had loved her idea. What was it again?

Baby pictures.

We were supposed to bring in baby pictures for a class online photo album.

I slid off the bed and climbed to my feet. I stretched my arms over my head, stretched my back. Yes. Good. A project. I needed a project to keep my mind away from my problems.

I made my way downstairs. I tried to think of where Mom and Dad might put the family photo albums. I knew they didn't like to keep their photos online. They printed their photos and kept them in albums.

But where were the albums?

Don't a lot of families keep their photo albums out where people can see them? Don't families like to look back and enjoy their old photos?

Where did my parents keep their albums?

I strode down the back hall and crept into my parents' bedroom. The room smelled of Mom's sweet, flowery perfume. The drapes were drawn, and it was dark in here. I clicked on the ceiling light.

The bed was made. Everything was in its place. It was obvious that Mom hadn't been home for a while. The papers on her desk in the corner were neatly stacked. The little couch that she usually covered in books and magazines was empty.

I stepped up to the tall bookcase against the far wall. It was filled with books, mostly hardcover novels and mystery stories. No framed photos anywhere. No albums.

I gazed around the room. Where were they?

I remembered that the room two doors down was used as a storage room. It had bookshelves from the floor to the ceiling on two walls. And it had a deep closet piled with old books and all kinds of junk.

My parents had two or three storage rooms like this. The old house had more rooms than our family needed. Dad kept promising he'd get them all fixed up, but we knew he never would.

Pale sunlight washed into the storage room from a high window, and a cloud of dust hung in the air. I used my phone as a flashlight to see better and beamed the light along the rows of books on the shelves.

No sign of any photo albums.

Finally, I found a couple of albums tucked away in the back of the deep closet. They were hidden behind my dad's college hockey uniform and a pile of torn and stained blankets.

I hoisted them both into my arms and carried them to my parents' bedroom. The covers were cracked and covered with a layer of dust that made me sneeze a couple of times.

I dropped them on the bed and sat beside them. I lifted the older-looking one onto my lap and began to turn pages. The photos looked yellowed and faded.

I flipped through page after page. I didn't recognize anyone in the book, not even my parents.

I was about to put this album down and try the other one—when a page caught my eye. I read the handwritten caption under a photo and gasped in shock.

And then a voice in front of me cried, *"What are you doing in here?"*

# 34

Freddy stood in the doorway, staring in at me.

"Photo albums," I said. "I found them." I motioned with both hands. "Freddy, come here."

He stepped into the room. "Are you going to bite me again?"

"No. I'm sorry," I said. "I got angry, that's all. I . . . I'm not feeling right."

He squinted at me. Hesitated.

"It's okay," I said. I slapped the bedspread. "Sit. Hurry."

For once, he obeyed. He plopped next to me on the edge of the bed.

"Look," I said, stabbing my pointer finger on a page of photos. "Is this weird or what?"

We both lowered our heads and gazed intently at the album.

At the top of the first page, my name was printed in blue ink: KATE.

And then, under the first photo, someone had printed: *Almost here.*

And the photo showed a close-up of an EGG.

Under the next photo, someone had printed in blue ink: *Can't wait to see my baby.*

That photo showed the same egg.

I flipped the page. We both stared at the next group of photos. Neither one of us said a word.

Freddy's name was at the top of this page. There were four photographs lined up perfectly. All four of them were photos of an egg.

I felt a chill at the back of my neck. My hands were suddenly cold and wet. I wanted to slam the album shut, but I couldn't stop staring at the eggs on the pages.

"Wh-what does this mean?" Freddy stammered. He jumped to his feet, his face twisted in confusion. "I mean, is it a joke or something?"

"I don't think so," I said softly. "I don't think it's a joke. But I don't know what it means."

I closed the album with trembling hands. My brain spun. I wanted to think of an explanation. But I couldn't think of a thing.

"We have to show this to Mom and Dad," Freddy said. "We have to ask them—"

Before he could finish, we heard a heavy *thud* in the hall outside the door. I jumped to my feet at the sound.

Another *thud* that seemed to make the floor shake.

Before Freddy or I could move, a huge creature burst into the doorway. It flicked a snakelike purple tongue at us. The lizard. The giant lizard, standing upright.

It filled the doorway, blocking out all the light from the hall. Its yellow eyes, bright as head-lights, slid from Freddy to me. It flicked its tongue again and clicked its enormous jaws.

And I screamed as it staggered heavily toward us, reached out its scaly green claws, and grabbed me by the shoulders.

# 35

I screamed again.

Freddy dove forward and bumped the lizard in the side. But Freddy wasn't strong enough to budge it.

The creature made horrifying panting sounds. Its tongue, sticky and warm, brushed over my face. Its claws held firmly to my shoulders.

Freddy tried to bump it away again, using his whole body. But the enormous, panting lizard was too big and too powerful. Freddy wrapped his arms around the creature's middle, and . . .

And . . .

The lizard raised its head, opened its jaws, and let out a room-shattering sneeze.

As I gaped at it, trembling in horror, its claws slid off me. It took a lumbering step back. And sneezed again.

The green slime from its nose splattered the wall.

The creature sneezed again. Again. Each violent eruption made the room shake.

"Sneezes like Dad," Freddy choked out.

And yes, as it sneezed, the lizard began to change. I stared in shock as its body began to shift.

I watched its claws pull in. Its snout melt into its face.

Another sneeze. Another snot splat against the wallpaper.

The lizard face sank into itself. The yellow eyes faded to black. As its scaly skin faded away, I could see human clothes beneath it. Khaki pants and a striped shirt.

And there was Dad.

Sneezing a last sneeze.

Dad, sweeping back his hair with one hand. Straightening his shirt. Beads of sweat on his forehead.

Dad shaking his head. "I'm so sorry," he said. "So sorry. I didn't mean to scare you."

Freddy and I were too stunned to move. We both stared openmouthed at him.

Dad took a few deep breaths. "So sorry. So sorry," he repeated. "I see you found the photo albums. I'm so sorry. Mom and I were waiting for the right time to tell you," he said.

Freddy squinted at him. "Tell us?"

Dad nodded. "Yes. Tell you that you weren't born—you were hatched."

Dad pushed the albums aside, and the three of us sat down side by side on the edge of the bed. "I wish your mom was here," he said, shaking his head. "She wanted to be here when we told you the truth about our family."

"Well, why is she still in Shaker Heights?" I asked.

He nodded. "She's helping your aunt hatch a new baby."

"Hatching a new baby? What's going on here, Dad? I don't get it at all," I said. I shook my head in disbelief. "Were you the huge lizard I saw in the lab? Standing at the worktable? That was *you*? And then you changed back?"

Dad nodded. He put an arm around my shoulders. "Yes, that was me. Our family isn't like most other families," he said softly.

"We're not people? We're lizards?" Freddy cried.

"Well . . . we're kind of both," Dad said.

Then he turned to me. "I'm really sorry I pretended I didn't know what you were talking about. I had to leave for Toronto, and I knew there wasn't time to explain everything."

I suddenly felt very angry. Dad should have explained. He shouldn't have run off to Canada without telling me.

"Let me explain now," he said. "First of all, when that Tasmanian cobra lizard bit you, Kate . . . That bite didn't harm you at all."

"It . . . it started to turn me into a lizard," I stammered.

Dad shook his head. "No, it didn't. The bite didn't do anything because you already *were* a lizard. All of us . . . Our whole family is shapeshifting lizards, Kate. We shift from human to lizard and back."

"But—but—" I sputtered. "Freddy doesn't act like a lizard. And I didn't act like a lizard until last week."

"Your lizard identity comes out when you are twelve or thirteen," Dad explained. "Freddy is too young."

Freddy suddenly went pale. "But I'll be a lizard in a couple of years?"

Dad chuckled. "Don't look so worried. You will both soon learn to control your lizard urges. You will be able to stay in your human form most of the time, just as I do."

"We can control it?" I asked.

"Yes. It will take practice," Dad replied. "But you will learn how to control when you shift and when you don't."

Dad opened the photo album and gazed at the photos of the eggs. A smile spread over his face. "You were such cute babies."

"Is this why you wanted a lizard farm?" Freddy asked. "Is this why you and Mom were so interested in lizards?"

"Yes," Dad said, still gazing at the egg photos. "Lizards are our ancestors and our relatives. I've always wanted to learn how this happened to our family."

I let out a long, sad sigh. "I'm having trouble with all this," I said. "I . . . I feel very upset and—and—"

"Listen to me," he said, squeezing my hands. "You'll be okay. You'll be able to control it. You can keep people from finding out. No one knows about your mom and me. No one. Kate, no one will know you come from a family of lizards."

I let out another long, miserable sigh. "Not true, Dad," I said, my voice cracking. "Not true. I'm ruined forever. I can't go back to school. I . . . I can't go anywhere."

A sob escaped my throat. "Everyone will know," I wailed. "I'll have no friends, no life at all. I'll be a total outcast. All alone. All alone forever."

Dad squeezed my hands again. "Stop," he

whispered. "Kate, don't say that. Why are you saying that?"

"Because of Adele!" I cried, my voice breaking again. "Adele Bender at school. Remember? She was here?"

"What about Adele?" Dad said.

"She has a video of me crawling on the gym floor after gym class. It shows me acting like a lizard, Dad. Adele says she's going to put it on YouTube so everyone can see it."

"Take a breath, Kate," Dad said. "You're trembling."

I took a deep breath and held it. But, of course, it didn't calm me down at all.

"Dad, she thinks as long as she has that video, she can get me to do whatever she wants. Like I'm her slave or something. I . . . I'll never be safe as long as she has that video. Never."

Dad placed his hands on my shaking shoulders. "Sssshhhh," he whispered. "Ssssh."

I took another deep breath. I could see that Dad was thinking hard.

"I think I can solve your Adele problem, Kate," he said finally. "I think I can solve it easily."

"Huh?" I blinked. "Seriously? How?"

# 37

"Invite Adele over," Dad said.

I squinted at him. "Huh? Invite her here? I don't think so."

A grin slowly spread across Dad's face. "Invite her over tonight, Kate." His eyes flashed. "Did you forget that we are carnivores?"

"Oh, gross," Freddy groaned.

He understood what Dad was saying before I did.

When I finally got it, I burst out laughing. Then Dad and I transformed into lizards. We both snapped our jaws and flicked our long tongues excitedly.

Adele showed up a little after five. I greeted her at the front door.

"Kate, you wanted to talk?" she said.

"Yes. Come in." I stepped aside so she could enter the house.

She sniffed the air and smiled. "Mmmm. What smells so good?"

"My dad is making a special sauce," I said.

Her smile faded quickly. "I guess you want to talk about the video I have?"

I nodded. "Yes. I do. Adele, come in. Take your coat off."

She frowned. "Why? Is this conversation going to take long?"

"Well . . ." I said. "Dad and I were hoping you could stay for dinner."

# 38

Did we really eat Adele for dinner?

That would be an awesome ending to my story, wouldn't it?

And it would definitely solve my problem with that video she had.

But the truth is, we didn't *have* to eat her.

Dad and I transformed into lizards. That scared Adele plenty. And then when we led her to the big roasting pot, bubbling with Dad's special tomato sauce, and we snapped our jaws hungrily, she got the point.

Victory was ours. Adele was shaking and quaking and stuttering and sweating. She begged us with her hands folded in front of her to take her off the dinner menu.

I guess the sauce didn't smell that great to her anymore. She was frightened enough to do whatever we asked. She took out her phone and deleted the video in front of our eyes.

Dad and I shifted back to being humans again.

Adele was still shaking and quaking. It was easy to get her to swear she'd never tell anyone about us.

So we let her go.

"Sorry I can't stay for dinner," she said. At that point, she would say *anything*. I never saw anyone run out of a house so fast.

"See you in school!" I shouted after her.

I knew Adele and I would never be friends. But at least now we understood each other.

As I joined Dad back in the kitchen, the only question that remained was what to have for dinner. And then we saw the two fat mice scamper under the pantry door.

## Welcome to SlappyWorld!

# SLAPPY BIRTHDAY TO YOU

## Here's a sneak peek!

**1**

On Ian Barker's twelfth birthday, he received a gift that brought pain and terror to him and his entire family.

But let's not get ahead of ourselves.

Let's try to enjoy Ian's birthday for as long as we can. Just keep in mind that it was not the birthday Ian had hoped for. In fact, it quickly became a day he would have given anything to forget.

Ian came down to breakfast on that sunny spring morning, eager for his special day to begin. Almost at once, he had trouble with his nine-year-old sister, Molly. But that was nothing new. If you ask Ian, "How do you spell *Molly*?" He'll answer, "T-R-O-U-B-L-E."

Since blueberry pancakes were Ian's favorite, Mrs. Barker had a tall stack of them on the table. Ian and Molly ate peacefully for a while. Molly liked her pancakes drowned in maple syrup, and she used up most of the syrup before Ian had a chance. But Ian didn't complain. He was determined to be cheerful on his birthday.

But then they came down to the last pancake on the platter. When they both stabbed a fork into it, that's when the t-r-o-u-b-l-e began.

"Mine," Ian said. "You've already had six."

"But I saw it first," Molly insisted. She kept her fork poking into her side of the pancake.

"It's my birthday," Ian reminded her. "I should get what I want today."

"You *always* think you should get what you want," Molly declared. Molly has wavy red hair and blue eyes, and when she gets into an argument about pancakes—or anything else—her pale, lightly freckled cheeks turn bright pink.

Their mom turned from the kitchen counter. She had been arranging cupcakes on a tray for Ian's birthday party. "Fighting again?"

"We're not fighting," Molly said. "We're *disputing*."

"Oooh, big word," Ian said, rolling his eyes. "I'm so totally impressed."

They both kept their forks in the last remaining pancake.

"You're a jerk," Molly said. "I know you know that word."

"Don't call Ian names on his birthday," Mrs. Barker said. "Wait till tomorrow." She had a good sense of humor. Sometimes the kids appreciated it. Sometimes they didn't. "Why don't you split the pancake in two?" she suggested.

"Good idea," Ian said. He used his fork to divide the pancake into two pieces.

"No fair!" Molly cried. "Your half is twice as big as mine."

Ian laughed and gobbled up his half before Molly could do anything about it.

Molly frowned at her brother. "Don't you know how to eat, slob? You have syrup on your chin."

Ian raised the syrup bottle. "How would you like it in your hair?"

Mrs. Barker turned away from the cupcakes and stepped up to the table. "Stop," she said. "Breakfast is over." She took the syrup bottle from Ian's hand. "You're twelve now. You really have to stop all the fighting."

"But—" Ian started.

She squeezed Ian's shoulder. "Your cousins are coming for your party. I want you to be extra nice to them and don't pick fights the way you always do."

Ian groaned. "Vinny and Jonny? They always start it."

"Ian always starts it," Molly chimed in.

"Shut up!" Ian cried.

"Just listen to me," Mrs. Barker pleaded. "I want you to be nice to your cousins. You know their parents have been going through a tough time. Uncle Donny is still out of work. And Aunt Marie is getting over that operation."

"Could I have a cupcake now?" Molly asked.

Ian slapped the table. "If she has one, I want one, too."

"Have you heard a word I said?" their mom demanded.

"I swear I won't start any fights with Jonny and Vinny," Ian said. He raised his right hand, as if swearing an oath. Then he stood up from his seat and started toward the cupcake tray.

"Hands off," Mrs. Barker said. "Go get your dad, Ian. Tell him the guests will be arriving soon."

"Where is he?" Ian asked.

"In his workshop," his mom answered. "Where else?"

"Where else?" Molly mimicked.

Ian walked down the back hall to the door to the basement. He thought about Jonny and Vinny.

Jonny and Vinny lived just a few blocks away. Jonny was twelve and Vinny was eleven, but they looked like twins. They were both big bruisers. Tough guys, big for their age, loud and grabby, with pudgy, round heads, short-cropped blond hair, and upturned pig noses.

At least, that's how Ian described them. The kind of guys who were always bumping up against people and each other, always giggling, always grinning about something mean. Mean guys.

"They're just jealous of you." That's what Mrs. Barker always told Ian. "They're your only cousins, so you have to be nice to them."

Ian opened the basement door and went down the stairs two at a time. The air grew warmer as he reached the basement, and it smelled of glue.

Under bright white ceiling lights, his father stood hunched over his long worktable. He turned as Ian approached. "Oh, hi, Ian."

"Hey, Dad," Ian started. "Mom says—"

"Here's a birthday surprise for you," Mr. Barker said. He reached both hands to his face, plucked out his eyes, and held them up to Ian.

Ian groaned. "Dad, you've been doing that joke since I was two. It just isn't funny anymore."

Mr. Barker tossed the eyeballs in the air and caught them. "You love it," he said. He set down the eyes and picked up a tiny arm and leg from the table. "You'd give an arm and a leg to do the eye joke as well as I do."

Ian laughed.

He gazed at the pile of arms and legs and other body parts on the long worktable. Broken dolls were piled at the other end. Doll heads stared wide-eyed at Ian as he surveyed his dad's work area.

Dolls stared down from shelves along two walls. Headless dolls. Dolls with eyes or arms or legs missing. A bucket beside the worktable was filled to the brim with yellow, red, and brown doll hair. There were shelves of dresses and pants and shirts and all kinds of new and old-fashioned doll clothing.

Ian's dad had started his doll hospital before Ian was born. He spent most every day down here, repairing the broken dolls, replacing missing parts, painting fresh faces, making old dolls look new. Then he carefully wrapped them and sent them back to their owners.

He picked up a slender paintbrush and began dabbing pale pink paint on a doll head's gray cheeks. "This is a vintage Madame Alexander Doll," he told Ian. "It's quite valuable, and when I received it, the face was completely rubbed off. So I—"

A hard knock on a door upstairs made him stop. Someone pounded the door four times, then four more.

"That's the front door," Mr. Barker said. "It must be your cousins. Go let them in." He squinted at the doll face and applied some more dabs with his paintbrush. "I'll be there in a few seconds."

Ian trotted up the stairs, then hurried down the hall toward the front door. He heard four more hard knocks. "I'm coming, I'm coming," he muttered.

Ian pulled open the front door—and let out a startled shriek as Jonny landed a hard-fisted punch in the middle of his face.

## About the Author

R.L. Stine's books are read all over the world. So far, his books have sold more than 300 million copies, making him one of the most popular children's authors in history. Besides Goosebumps, R.L. Stine has written the teen series Fear Street and the funny series Rotten School, as well as the Mostly Ghostly series, The Nightmare Room series, and the two-book thriller *Dangerous Girls*. R.L. Stine lives in New York with his wife, Jane, and Minnie, his King Charles spaniel. You can learn more about him at www.RLStine.com.

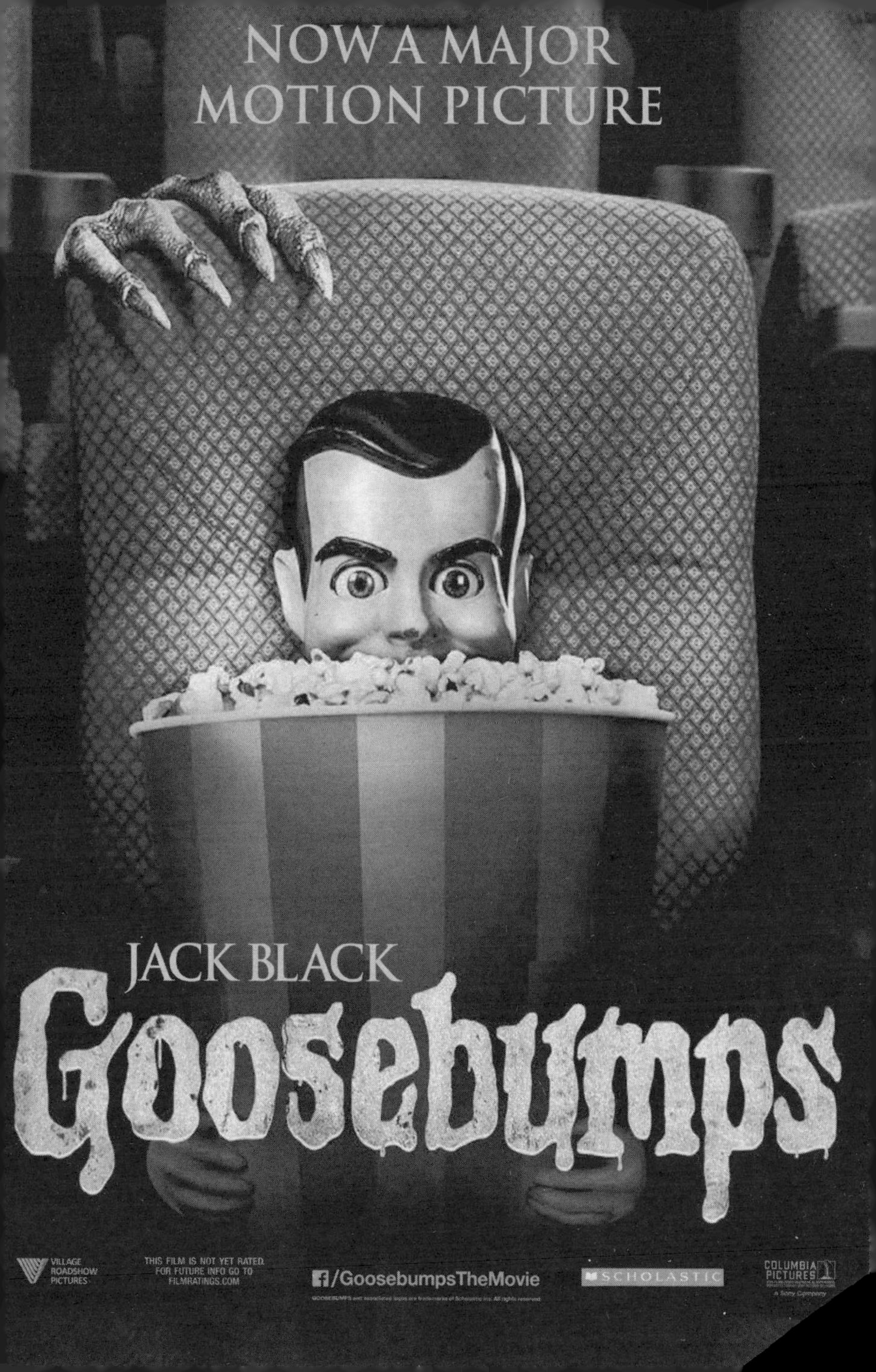

NOW A MAJOR
MOTION PICTURE
JACK BLACK
Goosebumps
VILLAGE
ROADSHOW
PICTURES
THIS FILM IS NOT YET RATED.
FOR FUTURE INFO GO TO
FILMRATINGS.COM
/GoosebumpsTheMovie
SCHOLASTIC
COLUMBIA
PICTURES
A Sony Company

# THE ORIGINAL Goosebumps BOOKS
## WITH AN ALL-NEW LOOK!

# THE SCARIEST PLACE ON EARTH!

# Catch the
# MOST WANTED
# Goosebumps® villains
# UNDEAD OR ALIVE!

## SPECIAL EDITIONS